THE

DEFECTOR

A Special Agent Dylan Kane Thriller

Also by J. Robert Kennedy

James Acton Thrillers

The Protocol	Blood Relics	Keepers of the Lost Ark
Brass Monkey	Sins of the Titanic	The Tomb of Genghis Khan
Broken Dove	Saint Peter's Soldiers	The Manila Deception
The Templar's Relic	The Thirteenth Legion	The Fourth Bible
Flags of Sin	Raging Sun	Embassy of the Empire
The Arab Fall	Wages of Sin	Armageddon
The Circle of Eight	Wrath of the Gods	No Good Deed
The Venice Code	The Templar's Revenge	The Last Soviet
Pompeii's Ghosts	The Nazi's Engineer	Lake of Bones
Amazon Burning	Atlantis Lost	Fatal Reunion
The Riddle	The Cylon Curse	The Resurrection Tablet
	The Viking Deception	

Special Agent Dylan Kane Thrillers

Rogue Operator	Black Widow	Extraordinary Rendition
Containment Failure	The Agenda	Red Eagle
Cold Warriors	Retribution	The Messenger
Death to America	State Sanctioned	The Defector

Templar Detective Thrillers

The Templar Detective	The Sergeant's Secret	The Black Scourge
The Parisian Adulteress	The Unholy Exorcist	The Lost Children
	The Code Breaker	

Kriminalinspektor Wolfgang Vogel Mysteries

The Colonel's Wife	Sins of the Child

Delta Force Unleashed Thrillers

Payback	Kill Chain	The Cuban Incident
Infidels	Forgotten	Rampage
The Lazarus Moment		Inside the Wire

Detective Shakespeare Mysteries

Depraved Difference	Tick Tock	The Redeemer

Zander Varga, Vampire Detective

The Turned

THE

DEFECTOR

A Special Agent Dylan Kane Thriller

J. ROBERT KENNEDY

UnderMill
PRESS

ISBN: 9781990418402

First Edition

For #10.

THE
DEFECTOR

A Special Agent Dylan Kane Thriller

"Loyalty to the country always. Loyalty to the government when it deserves it."

Mark Twain

"All Party members, service personnel, and other people should turn out as one with ardent loyalty to the Party and extraordinary patriotic zeal, and demonstrate the spirit and mettle of Korea that is rushing forward towards final victory racing against time."

Kim Jong-un
Supreme Leader of North Korea
2016 New Year Address

PREFACE

The Bridge of No Return has a storied history. It was once a key crossing between the two nations still technically at war, familiarly known as North and South Korea. After the signing of the Korean Armistice in 1953, it was used for prisoner exchanges, which is where it got its unofficial, ominous name. When a North Korean prisoner was brought to the bridge, they were given a choice: remain in South Korea, or cross the bridge into North Korea. If they chose the latter, they were told they could never return, even if they changed their minds. More than 100,000 prisoners of war were exchanged over this single bridge during Operation Little Switch, a test case, then Operation Big Switch.

In 1968, the illegally captured crew of the USS Pueblo were allowed to walk across the bridge after 11 months of captivity while a forced confession by the captain was played over loudspeakers.

But perhaps the most infamous event was in 1976 when two American soldiers attempting to trim a poplar tree blocking the view from a checkpoint were killed by North Korean soldiers in what became known as the Korean Axe Murder Incident. The North claimed the tree had been planted by the Supreme Leader himself and to cut it was sacrilege. In response, the Americans launched Operation Paul Bunyan, eventually felling the tree.

Two men dead over a tree.

And today, a man has parachuted onto this same bridge, in a move about to send a shockwave that will be felt around the entire world. An action with consequences far greater than the loss of a tree.

For once this man crosses the bridge, there can be no return.

Only death.

Bridge of No Return

Joint Security Area, North/South Korean Border

This was it. Less than one hundred feet to the rest of his life. This was no man's land, the demilitarized zone between North and South Korea where an uneasy peace reigned between two parties still technically at war. The South Korean guards behind him were still shouting at him to come back, but none dared take any action lest they provoke the always on-edge North Koreans at the other end of the bridge.

He was unarmed, his only defense against what might come his raised hands, his ballistic vest, and his demeanor. His heart beat a tad faster than usual, though that was expected. After all, he had just jumped from 50,000 feet and now stood on the most heavily guarded border in the world. He should be a little tense. But he was here by choice. This was what he wanted.

This was what he needed to do.

He slowly walked forward as lights trained on him from both sides, dawn just breaking minutes ago. While the South Koreans held their positions, North Korean soldiers emerged from behind their fortifications, aiming their Type 88-2 assault rifles at him, shouting for him to stop or they would shoot.

"I'm an American!" he announced, his voice calm and even, though raised.

"Hold your position or we will open fire!" was the immediate reply, the man on the speaker switching to English.

He stopped. "I need to speak to your commanding officer. I have urgent business with your government."

He was still several feet inside South Korea. Technically, they shouldn't shoot him until he crossed the line painted on the bridge, though the North Koreans were not known for their predilection for following the rules. They could shoot him right now, free of consequences, though he suspected once they figured out who they had shot, Pyongyang would torture and execute the shooter.

He was a valuable asset. Likely the most valuable to have made this crossing in years if not decades. The North Koreans would desperately want him. They just had to be given the opportunity to realize who was delivering himself into their hands.

A light armored vehicle pulled up, coming to an abrupt halt, a diminutive colonel exiting. The product of a lifetime of malnutrition fit his oversized hat in place then marched forward, a permanent scowl creasing his face. A guard rushed up to him, a whispered conversation held before the new arrival dismissed the man with a flick of his wrist. The colonel stepped forward then held his position at the start of the North Korean side of the bridge, flanked by four of his men.

"State your business!"

"I have urgent business with your government." He held up his hands and slowly turned. "As you can see, I am unarmed. May I approach?"

The man beckoned him forward and he slowly advanced, his hands still held high. This was the riskiest part. If he survived, the rest should be easy. They wouldn't dare harm an asset like him. He reached the colonel and extended a hand.

"I am CIA Operations Officer Dylan Kane, and I want to defect."

Leroux/White Residence, Fairfax Towers
Falls Church, Virginia

CIA Analyst Supervisor Chris Leroux lay in bed, exhausted. Some moron—Marc Therrien—had come into the office with the flu. When asked why, he said he didn't want to waste any sick days. Leroux had sent him home immediately, but the damage had been done. Half the team was sick before the end of the week, including him.

Therrien was healthy and back at work, but Leroux had been walloped. His fastidious ways and loner lifestyle pre-Sherrie meant he rarely got sick. His girlfriend, CIA Operations Officer Sherrie White, hadn't been ill a day since they had met. Part of her training was to avoid touching the mouth or nose with your hands, to wash them frequently, and to breathe through the nose whenever possible—all defenses against picking up a bug, natural or manmade.

He wasn't so careful, and wasn't accustomed to being this sick.

"How are you feeling?"

He groaned as Sherrie entered the bedroom with a tray carrying his lunch. "Like shit. Anyone who says they had the flu and it only lasted a few days has no idea what the flu is. They just had a cold." He shifted his position, propping up against the headboard. "What's on the menu?"

Sherrie placed the tray in front of him. "Tomato soup, grilled cheese sandwich, milk, orange juice, and me, if you're up for it."

He gave her a look. "I'm not up for it."

She laughed. "Thank God. You're icky!"

He flipped her the bird then sniffed the soup. It smelled wonderful. "I think my sinuses have cleared. I can actually smell that." He took a spoonful and gently blew on it before putting it in his mouth and swallowing. "And I can taste again. I might just be on the mend."

She sat on the edge of the bed and squeezed his shin. "You look a hell of a lot better than a few days ago."

"I thought I was icky." He took a bite of the cheddar and Swiss grilled cheese.

"You are. But two days ago you were super icky."

"Nice." He took another bite. It was good. So good. He was definitely feeling better.

"I have some bad news."

He continued to chew. "Don't care. Eating."

She giggled. "I have to head into the office. I just got a priority alert."

His eyes narrowed as he swallowed. "Something serious?"

She shrugged. "No idea. My handler wouldn't tell me anything, just that it was urgent I report in immediately."

Leroux's phone beeped a coded sequence, telling him a secure message had just been delivered through his best friend's private security network. He reached for his phone but Sherrie beat him to it.

"Dylan knows you're sick. He shouldn't be bothering you."

Leroux finished off the first half of his sandwich then washed it down with a large gulp of milk. "It's his secure network. It must be something serious."

"Serious to him."

"At least let me check."

She handed him the phone as she rose. "Fine. You'll just check the moment I leave anyway." She stripped bare then struck a pin-up pose. "You sure?"

Something stirred. He was *definitely* feeling better. "Well…"

"Ew!" She rushed into the bathroom and he laughed. He logged into the secure app then operated his phone with one thumb as he devoured the second half of his sandwich, his appetite returning with a vengeance.

Then he froze, midchew, as he read the message from his friend.

Tell Fang and my family that I am so sorry for what I have done, but I had no choice. I hope one day you can all forgive me.

"Sherrie!"

Sherrie bolted from the bathroom, concern on her face. "What?"

"Read this!" He held out the phone and she took it, her jaw dropping as she read the message.

"What the hell is this? What has he done?"

Leroux shook his head. "I have no idea. But it has to be something bad." He pushed the tray out of the way. "I have to go into the office."

Sherrie shook her head. "No, I'm going in already. I'll try to find out."

"He's my best friend. He's in some sort of trouble."

His phone vibrated in Sherrie's hand and she checked the display. "It's the Chief."

Leroux grabbed the phone and swiped his thumb. "Hey Chief. Is, umm, something going on with Kane?"

"How the hell did you find out so fast?"

Leroux's chest tightened and he squeezed his eyes shut. "Is he…alive?"

Sherrie gasped then rushed to the dresser, quickly pulling on clothes.

"We don't know. We assume so. If you're feeling up to it, I need my best man on this."

"I'm on my way."

"Only if you're up to it."

"I could have one foot in the grave and I'd still be coming in."

"Understood. I've already had your team activated. Sonya is setting up an ops center. Let me know when you arrive."

"Yes, sir."

The call ended and Leroux rolled out of bed, heading for the shower. "Something's wrong."

"What is it? Did he say?"

Leroux paused as he gripped the shower handle. "No, actually, he didn't. He just said he assumed Dylan was alive."

"You didn't ask?"

He sighed, turning the handle, the water rushing out of the showerhead. "I didn't think to ask." He stepped in and let the water soak him as Sherrie continued to prep at the vanity.

"*You* didn't think to ask? Are you sure you're ready to run an op?"

"I don't know, but I have to be there. If something's happened to Dylan, I can't just stay here. I have to do something. If I think I'm not up to it, I'll have Sonya take over and I'll just advise."

"Thank God for her. She's a godsend."

"She is." Leroux cursed. "Fang!"

"I'll go upstairs and tell her what's going on."

Leroux lathered up, enjoying the luxurious experience of bathing for the first time in days. "That should be a short conversation."

"Hopefully we'll know more later. We can both use the app to keep her informed."

"Be careful. If it involves Dylan, then it's going to be highly classified. We could make things worse for him if she finds out stuff she shouldn't."

"But he's basically her husband. She deserves to know."

"She deserves to know, but might not be cleared to know." He stepped in front of the stream and let the water rinse him off. "And you know her. She's ex-Special Forces. She's liable to do something stupid."

Sherrie groaned. "You're right, of course. God knows what I would do if I were in her situation and it was you who was in trouble."

"I would hope you'd break every damn law in existence to save me, as long as it didn't put your life at risk."

She pushed the shower curtain aside and smacked his ass. "I'd risk everything to save that tush."

He flexed the cheeks.

"Ooh, you are feeling better. Too bad we've got a friend to save."

"Too bad." He shampooed his hair as she returned to the sink. "Can you wait long enough for us to go in together?"

"Yes. I don't want you driving. I'm ready now, so I'm going to see Fang. Text me when you're ready."

"Sounds good."

Sherrie left and Leroux leaned against the wall, exhausted. He was definitely better, but he had no stamina. Sex with her would have killed him if his showering were any indication of his condition. His knees shook and he quickly rinsed his hair then turned off the shower. He carefully climbed out then grabbed a towel, heading directly for the bed. He sat on the edge and steadied his breathing.

He was in no condition to go into the office.

Yet he had to. Kane was his best friend, his only real friend. They had known each other since high school, and he couldn't turn his back on him now. No matter how sick he was.

He slowly toweled his hair dry then his body from his seated position. He eyed the tray of food for a moment then quickly finished it, every calorie of energy needed. His appetite was holding, a good sign, and he would need to continue to rebuild his strength throughout the day. He pushed to his feet and headed for the kitchen when he stopped.

They'll be happier to see me in clothes.

Kane/Lee Residence, Fairfax Towers
Falls Church, Virginia

Lee Fang, former Chinese Special Forces now exiled to the United States, sprinted as fast as she could on her treadmill. Her naked body rippled as every fiber of her sculpted frame was tasked to the limit with no clothes to chafe her skin or interfere with her performance.

It was a method of exercise she had adopted since coming to America, and the love of her life, Dylan Kane, would sometimes just watch her with a grin.

She loved that man.

Five years ago, she would have laughed in your face if it were suggested she would be living in America, in love with a white man. Yet here she was, hopelessly in love, in a country she now called home. While she missed China, and missed her family still trapped inside the Communist dictatorship, she could never imagine returning. She would love to see her family, of course, but it was too dangerous. She couldn't risk her life, nor theirs. A happy compromise had been struck after her departure, one never acknowledged on paper.

If she left China alone, China would leave her and her family alone.

That, of course, had been an agreement broken recently, but since then, the uneasy truce seemed to be holding. She would have to be happy with her new family, content in the knowledge her old one was safe. Kane was a man she could see spending the rest of her life with, and could even see them getting married eventually, though that meant official records, and they both kept low profiles.

She didn't need a ring or a certificate to tell her who she loved, or who loved her.

Her timer beeped and she reduced the speed, beginning her cooldown, when there was a knock at the door. She frowned. She wasn't expecting anyone, and she made it a point to not associate with the neighbors, except, of course, for Sherrie and her boyfriend who lived in the same building a few floors down.

The knock persisted then her phone chimed.

She grabbed it and read the message from Sherrie.

It's me. Answer the door!

Fang yanked the safety clip out of the treadmill, bringing it to a halt. She grabbed her shorts and slipped them on, then shrugged into her sports bra, both sitting nearby just for such an occasion. She snatched a towel and headed for the door as the knocking continued, wiping the sweat off her body. She opened the door and Sherrie barged in.

"Oh, thank God! I was beginning to think you weren't home."

Fang was immediately concerned at her friend's state. "What's wrong?"

"Come." Sherrie led her into the apartment then pushed her onto the couch, taking a seat beside her. "Now, I don't want you to read too much into this, but something is going on with Dylan."

Fang tensed, her stomach flipping. "Tell me everything you know."

"Not much. I've been called in urgently. I don't know if it's related, but I have a feeling it is. Dylan sent a secure message over his private network to Chris just a few minutes ago. It said something along the lines of, 'Tell Fang and my family that I'm sorry for what I've done, but I had no choice. I hope you can forgive me someday.' I'm paraphrasing, but you get the gist. Then, a few minutes after that, the Chief called asking if Chris could come in, and when Chris asked if Dylan was alive, the Chief said they assume so." Sherrie held up a hand, cutting off Fang's obvious question. "No, Chris didn't think to ask what was going on, and the Chief probably wouldn't have told him. If it involves Dylan, it must be something serious, and it's definitely classified."

Fang squeezed her eyes shut for a moment, stemming the tears that threatened to flow. Something had happened to her beloved, but she had to keep a level head. If Langley believed he was still alive, it meant they had no evidence to suggest he was dead. It meant there was still hope, and these people were the best in the world. If anyone could save him, it was the CIA. She opened her eyes, blinking away the tears. "Is that all you know?"

Sherrie frowned. "I'm afraid so. We'll know more soon, but depending on how compartmentalized it is, we might not be able to share anything with you. Just know that Chris is heading in with me now, and you know him. He won't stop at anything to save Dylan."

Fang's shoulders shook. Just once. Sherrie was right. Leroux would do everything he could, but sometimes that just wasn't enough. "Tell me what you can when you can," she murmured.

Sherrie gave her a hug, a hug she didn't return, then rose. "I have to go. One of us will try to get in touch with you as soon as we know something we can share."

Fang nodded. "I'll be here."

Sherrie gave her a compassionate frown then headed out, nothing more needing to be said. Fang rose then headed for the shower, her mind a tumult of emotions and unanswered questions, and worse, brutal imaginings of what might be happening to the only man she had ever truly loved.

She stepped into the shower and stood under the water, letting it wash over her, then collapsed in the corner, sobbing uncontrollably as she remembered the last time he had been home and the shower they had shared.

Please let him be all right.

Operations Center 2, CIA Headquarters

Langley, Virginia

CIA Senior Analyst Sonya Tong sat at her station, staring at the massive display that curved across the front of the state-of-the-art operations center buried in the bowels of CIA Headquarters. And she couldn't believe what she was looking at.

It couldn't be real.

The footage showed a man parachuting onto the Doraol Su Eomneun Dari Bridge between North and South Korea, then calmly walking to the North's side of the border and surrendering to them before being driven away—not in handcuffs, but with a handshake.

And that person was Dylan Kane.

"This is bullshit!"

Tong had to agree with their tech wunderkind, Randy Child, as he spun in his chair, staring up at the ceiling. "It may be." She turned to the team, in charge until Leroux arrived. "I want this footage analyzed for anything unusual. Is it a deepfake? Is there any indication it's someone else in disguise? Check his mannerisms against archival footage. Everything. We need to know if one of our top operatives just handed himself over to the North Koreans."

"What if he did?" asked Marc Therrien, one of the team's most seasoned analysts. "What are we going to do? The things he knows…"

Tong exhaled loudly as she slowly shook her head. "I don't know."

"We kill him, don't we?"

The room gasped at Child's statement and he held up a hand, cutting off any verbal assault.

"Just hold up a sec before you try and tear me a new one. I'm not saying that's what I want to have happen, I'm just saying, in these situations, where it looks like they're clearly a traitor, don't we try to kill them before they can reveal too many secrets?"

Tong bit her lip. "Yes, it's been done, but this doesn't make sense. Why would he defect to North Korea of all places?" She pursed her lips. "Start pulling all his mission reports. Let's find out any connection he has to North Korea. Missions, contacts, anything, no matter how remote. There has to be a reason he went there."

The door hissed open and she breathed a relieved sigh then suppressed a gasp of concern as Leroux entered looking like hell. He had been sick with the flu, and he was worried—she could see it in the poor dear's eyes. Greetings were called to him from the others, and he weakly waved at them as he dropped into his chair at the center of the room, adjusting his mask.

"Thanks, people. Yes, I feel like shit, which is why I'm doing you the courtesy of wearing a mask. I wouldn't have come in"—he gave a look at Therrien who shrunk behind his monitor—"but with this being Dylan, well…you know."

"Glad you're here," said Tong. "The Chief wants to see you right away."

Leroux's shoulders slumped. "Ugh. Fine. Give me a second to catch my breath. I didn't realize how weak I was until I walked from the parking garage to here." He motioned at the footage cycling on the display. "What am I looking at?"

"Footage from the South Korean side of the Doraol Su Eomneun Dari Bridge, 6:32 a.m. local."

Leroux squinted. "Wait a minute. You mean this happened last night our time?"

"Yes."

"Then why are we just hearing about it now?"

"The South Koreans shared the footage as part of the daily brief, which takes place at eight each morning our time. It took a few hours to work its way up the chain once facial recognition ID'd him."

"So, he's been there since last night. Have the North Koreans said anything?"

"Not that I'm aware of. The Chief might know more." She lowered her voice slightly, leaning toward him. "This is huge, Chris. I mean, it's Dylan! It's like James Bond defecting. What are we going to do?"

Leroux closed his eyes for a moment and her heart broke for him. This was his best friend in the world, someone no one in the room could imagine betraying his country. Leroux rose as he opened his eyes. "We find out the truth. Something has to be going on here. If he's

19

turned traitor, then the Chief will take appropriate action. Right now, all evidence suggests he's a traitor and a team might be assigned to take him out. I refuse to believe that, so it's up to us to determine the truth before a hit squad is sent in to take out my friend." His voice cracked and he squeezed his eyes shut as he leaned forward, his knuckles white against the desktop. "I'm sorry. I'm a little too close to this, which is probably why the Chief brought me in. He knows I won't stop until I prove Dylan's innocence."

"You can count on us," said Therrien from the back of the room, everyone agreeing.

Child shrugged. "I already said it was bullshit. I don't know him like you do, but there's no way in hell that dude would betray his country. No damned way."

Ministry of State Security Headquarters

Pyongyang, North Korea

"My name is Dylan Kane. I'm an operations officer in the Central Intelligence Agency's Special Operations Group based out of Langley, Virginia. My handler is Beverly Thorn and my supervisor is Director Leif Morrison, National Clandestine Service Chief."

Major Pak Ryong-hae sat across the table from what might be the most valuable intelligence asset his glorious nation had seen in decades. This man, if he were who he claimed, was without a doubt the most important thing to happen in Pak's career.

That meant he couldn't screw it up.

Pyongyang would have his head if something went wrong here. And it could go wrong in so many ways. This man might be an imposter, pretending to be Dylan Kane. Dylan Kane might be a plant by the CIA or another clandestine organization, placed here to feed them false intel. Or he might be the genuine article, disillusioned with his failing country and desiring a fresh start in the greatest nation this planet had ever known.

It could make, or break, his career.

He had to be careful.

"Why are you here?"

"As I said before, I wish to defect."

"Why? I thought America was supposed to be the greatest country in the world. Why would you want to leave that?"

"Because America is a lie. The country is divided into two warring camps that hate each other so much, they're willing to destroy their country so the other side can't have it. It's only a matter of time before it turns into a civil war, and I don't want to be there for that. America had its chance to be the peacemakers, to be the shining example to the rest of the world, but they've blown their shot. It's time for a new way of thinking where dissension among the population isn't tolerated, where those who would tear down what has been built aren't tolerated."

"And you believe the Democratic People's Republic of Korea is that new way of thinking?"

"Democracy has failed. The idea of giving every person a vote means every idiot gets to vote. There are very few countries in the world that aren't democracies that also aren't dominated by religion, mostly Islam, or aren't trying to have their cake and eat it too."

Pak eyed the man. "Cake?"

"It means they want the best of both worlds. Take China. They are a Communist state but are too capitalist. They've abandoned their principals. So has Cuba, so has Vietnam. Only North Korea has stuck to its guns. You guys have a single leader who rules with an iron fist, and if anyone defies him, they're dead. I respect that. It's absolute rule. And you haven't embraced the capitalist ways like China has. That only leads to democracy and to the mess we have back in the US. And when my country descends into civil war, it will create a vacuum that countries like China and Russia will attempt to fill."

"And North Korea."

"Yes, but to a lesser extent. Let's be honest, you don't have the military power or the capabilities."

Pak bristled at the insult, and his subject picked up on it.

"That's not your fault, and really, that's why I'm here. I know things. I know a *lot* of things. I can help you in your weapons development programs. Rockets, nuclear weapons, submarines, pretty much anything."

This was the first thing that the man had said that Pak didn't believe. Nobody knew everything. "I don't believe anyone can be an expert in all these things. I think you are telling me what you think I want to hear."

The man chuckled, dismissing the concern with a wave of his hand. "You're right, I'm not. I'm a bit of an expert on a lot of things. What I know is *who* knows."

Pak stared at the man. "What do you mean?"

"My job means I know who the experts are. If you want an expert on rockets, I know the experts. If you want an expert on nuclear weapons, I know who you need. I can give you names, locations, and help you defeat any security they might have." He leaned forward. "I can fill that International Cooperation Center of yours with anyone you need on any subject. You name it, and I'll provide it."

Pak leaned back, regarding the man. He had mentioned the International Cooperation Center, the ICC. It was a secret location where defectors and "volunteers" had been recruited to work for the benefit of the state. It wasn't out of the question that this man would know of its existence. All it indicated was that he was well-informed. "International Cooperation Center?"

The man smiled. "Don't play stupid with me, Major. We both know what I'm talking about. Nice little complex you've got surrounded by neat little houses straight out of the sixties for your so-called guests."

Pak shifted slightly in his chair. "You could have read that off the Internet."

"I could have, but I didn't need to. I've been there."

Pak laughed. "That, I highly doubt."

"Ask your superiors about what happened there a few years back. You kidnapped three American scientists and their families. Two scientists somehow escaped with their families, and the third destroyed your lab with an EMP then was killed by a sniper before you could torture him."

Pak eyed him suspiciously. "And how do you know this?"

"I was that sniper." The man folded his arms and leaned back. "Now, how about we get someone who can make a deal in here. If I'm not who I say I am, how would I know what happened at your International Cooperation Center? I broke them out and put them on a submarine that got them safely home. If you want more details, then fine. But let's get real here. I'm offering to help you. I can advance your weapons programs by decades. I have secrets about my country and its allies that will have your leaders giggling with glee. The dirt I have can topple governments or have them offering you whatever you want to keep silent. All you have to do is trust me."

Pak drew a slow breath. "And that is the question, sir, can we trust you?"

"Test me."

"Oh, we will. But what is it you want?"

"Not much. A nice house, access to my money on the outside, some lady friends, Internet access, unfettered access to banned imports—"

"It sounds like you want to live an American lifestyle, not a Korean one."

He smiled. "I want to live like your elite does, not your citizens. They have everything I just described. I will even fund it with my own money. All I want is permission. And in exchange, I'll get you whatever scientists you need so that when America collapses, your country will be ready to capitalize on the vacuum created."

Pak stared at the man. The facts he had laid out regarding the events at the ICC were easy enough to check on. There had been whispered references made to it over the years, but like most things here, when something went wrong, it was covered up. If this was the man responsible, it could mean death, though it might prove he was who he said he was.

An extremely valuable asset.

Pak had never been to the ICC but he was well aware of it. It was an essential part of his country's successes over the decades, and if this man could help recruit more "volunteers"—even he was amused by that—his country could benefit a lot. And all that was needed was to allow this man to live here as one of the elite, on his own funds, while he rode out the collapse of his own nation—something long predicted by the great leaders that had ruled them.

American and Western decadence and greed would be their downfall.

And apparently, it was finally happening.

"I'll take your requests to my superiors. They'll determine what to do with you."

"And in the meantime?"

"You'll get a taste of what awaits you should you be lying."

"I don't think I like the sound of that."

"You shouldn't."

Director Morrison's Office, CIA Headquarters

Langley, Virginia

"You look like shit."

Leroux dropped into a chair in front of Director Morrison's desk, feeling as described. "I guess it's official then. My team agrees with you."

Morrison chuckled though regarded him with concern. "Are you sure you're well enough to be here? If Dylan has indeed defected, then there's not much we can do in the next twenty-four hours. Another day of rest might do you good."

Leroux shook his head. "No, I have to be here, working the problem."

"And what do you see as the problem?"

"That there's something else going on here. There's no way Dylan has defected. It's impossible. But…"

"But?"

Leroux pulled out his phone and brought up the message, handing it over to his boss. Morrison read it, his eyebrows climbing, and he cursed as he returned the device. "I want a copy of that."

"Yes, sir."

"That seems to confirm it, though, doesn't it?"

"On the surface."

"Explain."

"Well, if he wanted to make his story convincing, he'd want us to all react in just the way we are."

"Which is?"

"Shocked. Surprised. Panicked."

"So, what do you suggest?"

"Let my team do its job. Prove it one way or the other."

Morrison pursed his lips and said nothing as he stared at Leroux. Leroux shifted in his chair. "There's something you need to know."

Leroux tensed as the other shoe was about to drop. "What?"

"I received a message from Dylan as well. It was sent the moment we received the footage."

"What did it say?"

Morrison put on his glasses then tapped at his phone. "It says, 'If you're going to kill me, send the best you've got otherwise the blood will be on your hands.'"

Leroux's shoulders sagged. "Are we reading this all wrong? I mean, could he have actually defected?"

Morrison tossed his glasses on his desk. "Every single piece of evidence we have suggests that he has. I have no choice but to assume he actually has, and that means there's only one course of action I can follow."

"Termination."

"Exactly. He knows too much. I have no choice but to send in a team to take him out."

"That's a high-risk operation, sir. He'll be held in a high-security area, for sure. Getting in will be difficult."

"Yes, it is, which is why I want your team trying to determine what is really going on. In the meantime, I'm putting a team in to take him out. You have until they're in position to prove me wrong."

Leroux closed his eyes. "Who are you sending in?"

"I'm taking Dylan's advice. I'm sending in the best we've got."

"Who?"

"Bravo Team."

Vander, North Carolina

"Here you go, little man."

Sergeant Carl "Niner" Sung's eyes bulged as the sonofabitch of a friend tossed a box at him from the back of the moving van. He caught it square in the chest like the shock from a defibrillator, and promptly fell on his ass on the pavement. "Ow!"

Sergeant Leon "Atlas" James snickered. "I thought you said you could carry anything I could carry."

Niner pushed the box off his chest and onto the driveway before rubbing at his now sore ribs. "I said carry, not catch!" He rose and brushed off. "What the hell was in that thing?"

Atlas shrugged. "Books, I think."

"You threw a box of books at me?"

"And you caught them like a girly man. Did I bruise your ego?"

"You bruised my ribs." Niner rubbed his butt. "And my ass. I'm going to have Angela check me out tonight, and if there's any damage to this perfect specimen, I'm sending photos."

"I don't want to see your bruised ass."

"I'm not sending them to you. I'm sending them to your girlfriend."

"She's not going to want to see that narrow little ass of yours either."

Niner's girlfriend, Angela Henwood, stepped out onto the porch of Sergeant Will "Spock" Lightman's in-laws' new home. "Are you two fighting again?"

Niner dropped his pants and aimed his ass in her direction. "Look what he did to me!"

Angela batted a hand. "You two really need to get a room and put the question to rest once and for all."

Atlas' girlfriend, Vanessa Moore, joined her. "What now?" She cringed as she raised a hand to block the view. "Niner! Put that thing away!"

Niner pointed a finger at Atlas. "He started it."

"I don't care. If you two don't get back to work, I'm gonna finish it. Now pull your pants up before you get a spanking."

Niner grinned. "Told you she wanted to see it. Now she wants to touch it."

Atlas shook a fist. "Pants up or I'm strapping you to the top of the truck and leaving you there."

"You always want to tie me up. I think she's right. Let's get a—"

Atlas held up a finger. "Don't you dare say it."

Command Sergeant Major Burt "Big Dog" Dawson emerged from the house with Spock. "Niner! Pants up! We've got boxes to move!"

Niner pulled up his pants then picked up the box of books, tossing them to Spock with a grunt. Spock caught the box easily, an eyebrow cocked.

"Is this how you treat my in-laws' things?"

Niner stabbed his finger at Atlas again. "He started it."

"Don't make me finish it!" yelled Vanessa from inside the house.

Dawson laughed as he hopped into the back of the truck and handed out several more boxes before jumping down and grabbing another left at the edge of the door. They all filed into the house, Spock's mother-in-law directing them after reading each label. Niner headed upstairs with his box, narrowly avoiding a collision with Spock's excited daughter as she rushed down the stairs, clearly delighted about the room that would be hers when she stayed here.

Spock's wife Joanne had been killed recently in an attack by the Russian mob, and while retribution had been taken, nothing was bringing her back. Spock had talked it out with the family, and Joanne's parents had agreed to move closer to Fort Bragg so they could watch their granddaughter while Spock was deployed. It allowed him to stay in the Unit and provide a stable home for his daughter while he was out protecting her and her country from those who would do them harm.

They were 1st Special Forces Operational Detachment—Delta, commonly known to the public as Delta Force, and the entirety of Bravo Team was here today helping with the move. It had been hours, but they were almost done, and it was worth it to keep their friend as part of the team. There had been some doubt in Nigeria about whether he would stay on, but the mission had convinced him the work he was doing was necessary.

Niner couldn't imagine how difficult a decision it must have been. He didn't have children, though Angela had indicated she'd like some eventually. It was too soon for an honest talk about that, but now that the relationship was serious, and appeared to be heading in the right direction, these things needed to be discussed in general—there was no point in wasting a year or two together to find out they wanted fundamentally different things.

He wanted children. Lots of them, though two would probably be enough of a handful. Whatever they were blessed with, he'd be happy. He just wanted a family. Desperately now that it was in sight. He had resigned himself long ago to dying a bachelor—he just wasn't good with women. But Angela made it so easy. She got his sense of humor and enjoyed it rather than just tolerated it. And he could be himself around her without always being the class clown.

He wanted to start planning a future that included a wife and kids.

He was ready to settle down.

But he still wanted to kick ass for his country—he couldn't see that changing any time soon.

"Anybody home?"

Niner gave Spock a confused look, the widower's eyebrow shooting up to his hairline. "Is that the colonel?"

"Yes, sir!" shouted Spock as he rushed down the stairs to greet their commanding officer. "Sir, you're always welcome, but I didn't expect you to help with the move."

Colonel Thomas Clancy chuckled as Niner joined the growing group of warriors at the front door. "I'm afraid I'm here on business, gentlemen, not moving duty." Clancy turned to Dawson. "Sergeant Major, I need to have a word with you. In private."

"Yes, sir." Dawson stepped out of the house with Clancy then turned. "Hold off on the beer until I get back."

A round of exaggerated complaints followed him out the door and Niner turned to the others. "Well, we better get this done quickly. When the colonel shows up personally, you know it can't be good."

Operations Center 2, CIA Headquarters
Langley, Virginia

Leroux entered the operations center and the team fell silent as all eyes turned to him. He dropped into his chair, exhausted, then turned to his team with a heavy heart. "I just met with the Chief and it isn't good. Dylan messaged him as well."

"What did he say?" asked Tong, her voice gentle.

"He basically told the Chief to send the best we've got to take him out, otherwise any blood will be on the Chief's hands."

"Holy shit!" muttered Therrien from the back of the room, the others murmuring their shock as well.

"The Chief is dispatching Bravo Team to take him out. Unless we can prove Dylan is innocent before they're in position, they'll execute their orders."

Child cursed as he spun in his chair. "Which means they execute him."

"Yes." Leroux sighed. "Have we found anything?"

Tong nodded. "We found out how he got on the bridge. He chartered a plane then jumped in from high altitude. It allowed him to skirt the civilian no-fly zone and land on the bridge, bypassing Southern security."

"And prove to his new hosts what he's capable of, lending credence to any story he tells them."

Tong lowered her voice and leaned closer to him. "I had a thought."

Leroux pushed his chair closer with his foot. "What?"

"You said you got a message from Dylan, and now the Chief has as well."

"Yes."

"Well, you both received them after he was identified in the footage provided by the South Koreans."

"Right. Your point?"

"Well, how is he sending them? I mean, even if they end up believing him, there's no way they've let him keep his phone. He can't be the one sending the messages."

Leroux's jaw dropped at the obvious revelation. She was right, and the fact it hadn't occurred to him was further confirmation he wasn't ready to be running an op.

His stomach rumbled. He was hungry again, another indicator his body was on the mend despite his mind wallowing in fog.

Tong smiled. "You should go to the cafeteria and get something to eat. I'll have the team start tracing those messages. We need to find out not only how he's sending them, but also how whoever or whatever is sending them knows when to."

Leroux stood. "Good thinking. Take over for a while. I'm going to get some food then a few hours rack time. I'm useless."

"Don't worry. I've got you covered."

He flashed her a grateful smile through his mask and headed for the door. "Sonya's in charge until I return." He groaned as he stepped out into the hall. "*If* I return."

I'm totally weak.

Ministry of State Security Headquarters
Pyongyang, North Korea

He could fake it, but to what end? He was here to prove he was Dylan Kane, super-spy, and pretending to be exhausted, to giving in to their interrogation techniques, would simply demonstrate he wasn't who he said he was. They would know he had been trained for situations like this, and sleep deprivation and bright lights would do little to break him.

He had to have patience, and everything would work out. For now, he was in a cold, damp cell in the basement of the Ministry of State Security Headquarters used for people like him. They hadn't laid a finger on him, but everything was loud here. Every cell door that opened or shut was done with gusto. Boot heels slammed on concrete floors with extra vigor. All orders were shouted.

It was impossible to sleep.

Unless you were trained.

So, he slept like a baby.

He was still a little jetlagged, though he had been in South Korea for two days making the final arrangements for his defection. The several hours of restful sleep he managed while he waited to hear his fate from his captors-soon-hosts was only interrupted by a nightmare involving Fang. She was what he would miss the most while here. There was no hope of bringing her here due to her status with North Korea's greatest ally, China. And he'd miss Leroux and the others as well, and obviously his family. It was a major sacrifice, but worth it.

It better be worth it.

He was giving up a lot by doing this, not to mention risking his neck. If the North Koreans decided he was full of shit, or not worth the bother, he'd be dead, though not before days, weeks, or even months of torture.

Footfalls echoed then came to a halt on the other side of the cell door. He sat up, straightening himself as the key hit the lock, the mechanism clicking loudly like everything else here, and Major Pak entered.

Kane stood. "So, what's the verdict?"

Pak frowned. "They don't believe you."

"That's not good. What can I do to convince them?"

"You will be interrogated by specialists over the coming days. You will tell them everything they want to know, and they will be verifying everything you say. A single lie, and you die. Slowly."

Kane rolled his eyes. "That's amateur stuff and you know it. Don't ask me your standard questions. I'm a spy, my knowledge is highly compartmentalized for a reason. I can't tell you the names of other assets or operatives inside your country, or ways to hack Langley, because I don't need to know those things. I'm given a mission with very narrow parameters and just enough intel for me to succeed. That's it. But, over the years, I've made it my business to know who knows what in case I ever need a question answered. And quite often those people are not known to the public, and you can't just call them up. You have to beat their security then talk to them in person."

Pak regarded him skeptically. "And I'm sure they're willing to talk to some stranger who broke into their home or office because of his winning smile?"

Kane laughed and wagged a finger at Pak. "I like you. I think in time we'll be friends. But to answer your question, yes, they are quite willing to talk. They're usually isolated, alone, and only have their work. They're thrilled to talk to someone on the outside. America and its allies have hundreds if not thousands of these people working for them in top-secret facilities around the world, working on things you couldn't possibly imagine. And I can give you access to them." He tapped his chin. "How about this? Forget interrogating me under bright lights. I could screw with you for days and you'd never know. Instead, test me. Let me get you someone you need, and that will prove not only my worth, but my sincerity."

Pak pursed his lips, staring at him. "And just who did you have in mind?"

Kane smiled. "You have a failed nuclear power program, don't you?"

Pak shifted slightly. "What makes you think it is a 'failed' program?"

"You don't have a single functioning plant despite working on this since the fifties. I'd say that's a failed program."

Pak lowered his voice slightly. "If you intend to make this your home, you must learn to *never* refer to any state program as failed."

Kane smirked. "Politics. I understand that. The thesaurus aside, how about I tell you the exact person you need to jumpstart your program, and how to get him here." He leaned in closer. "Tomorrow."

Vander, North Carolina

"Let's take your car, but I'm driving."

Dawson laughed at Clancy's statement. "Never lose that sense of humor, sir."

Clancy chuckled and headed for the passenger seat of Dawson's pride and joy, his 1964½ Mustang convertible in original poppy red, inherited from his father. He loved this car and babied it like she deserved to be.

And nobody drove it but him.

He climbed in the driver's seat and started the engine, giving the throttle a little extra shove, enjoying the roar. "Top up or down, sir?"

"Leave it down. There's a reason I wanted to take your car. I've always wanted a convertible, but my wife nixed the idea. I tell ya, if she goes first, I'm heading to the dealership on my way home from the funeral."

"Don't tell her that, sir." Dawson eased them from the curb and headed in no particular direction. This wasn't the first time the colonel had asked him on a ride, and he was certain it wouldn't be the last. All he did know was that every time it happened, it wasn't good news. Dawson reached around and grabbed a ballcap off the floor of the back seat. "Better put this on, sir, you'll burn."

Clancy fit the Army cap in place, but not before running his fingers through his thinning hair. "Thanks, Sergeant Major." Clancy said nothing as BTO gently played on a perpetually tuned station from the factory-original AM-only radio. "Good tune."

"Yes, sir. Nothing but the classics played in this classic."

"It would be sacrilege to play the shit the kids listen to today in a fine automobile like this."

Dawson grunted. "Don't get me started, sir. Half the guys in the Unit are in their twenties. I swear some of them don't know what a song sounds like without Auto-Tune or an f-bomb every second verse."

They pulled out of the residential area and Dawson had them heading into the country so no stray words could be heard. He waited for the colonel to broach the subject.

Clancy leaned back in his seat and closed his eyes for a moment before sighing heavily. "I have some bad news."

Dawson tensed. "What?"

"Dylan Kane just defected to North Korea."

"What?" Dawson's jaw dropped as he stared at his commanding officer. "Are you sure?"

"Eyes on the road, Sergeant Major."

Dawson returned his attention to the road but didn't have to adjust his steering, his training leaving him always aware of precisely where his vehicle was heading. "Sir, what can you tell me?"

"Everything I know. You're being retasked to the CIA. Two teams. One will enter North Korea, the other will be offshore to assist should it become necessary."

Dawson's stomach knotted. "What are our orders?"

"Your orders are to locate and eliminate Kane before he reveals everything he knows to one of our greatest enemies."

Dawson shook his head. "This is bullshit. There's no way he defected. It makes no sense."

"That's what I said when Director Morrison called me personally."

"But he was one of us. He was a member of my team. I know him. There's no way in hell he's defected."

"A lot of people agree with you, but he parachuted onto the Bridge of No Return then calmly walked over to the North Korean side and was welcomed with a handshake and a drive. Then there are the messages."

"Messages?"

"He apparently sent messages to Morrison and Leroux. Leroux's was an apology, and Morrison's was a challenge."

"Challenge?"

"He basically said that if Morrison was going to kill him, he better send his best, otherwise their blood would be on his hands."

"So, they're sending us."

"Yes."

Dawson bit his lip as he stared ahead. "Was anyone else considered for the mission?"

"Not that I'm aware of. Your team is the best and has worked with the CIA too many times to count. They know you, they know what you're capable of."

"But they have their own teams."

"Yes, but there's concern they might have a mole."

Dawson's eyebrows shot up. "A mole?"

"The messages were sent precisely when the CIA identified Kane as the man in the footage. There's no way he could have known because he was already in custody, and the identification didn't happen until the next day. Someone triggered those messages. If they have a mole, then they're concerned any team they send in might be compromised, or the North Koreans might be notified."

"Who's Control?"

"Leroux's team initially. They're being sequestered now. All communications monitored and no leaving the ops center without an escort until the mission is complete. When the kill order is issued, another team with no connection to Kane will take over."

Dawson's eyes narrowed. "If they're taking that precaution from the CIA side of things, why not us? We're about the only team at Bragg that has a deep connection with Kane. He's a brother."

"I argued that, but Morrison insisted. I believe he is still holding out hope that this is some sort of misunderstanding, and he wants fingers on those triggers that will think rather than just act."

"Are you saying we should question the order when it comes?"

Clancy regarded him. "Not at all. I'm saying use your best judgment. What the eye in the sky says is happening might not be what the eye on the scope sees. If you have that shot and are ordered to take it, but your gut tells you something else is going on, then make your own decision." He smirked. "Just don't tell them I told you."

"I never would, sir."

"Bullshit. If it turns into a Charlie-Foxtrot because you don't take the shot, you tell them I told you not to. Don't fry your career because I planted doubt. I don't mind going down for it. I can retire at any time if I want to. You've still got a promising career ahead of you."

Dawson pursed his lips. "Are you thinking of retiring?"

"We all do at my age, but if I did, who the hell would cover your ass when you took dangerous advice?"

"Like they say, no one can replace you, sir, only succeed you. But don't stick around for us. You deserve your retirement."

Clancy grunted. "My wife just told me on the way to see you that her sister has suggested she might move in with us since she's having some mobility issues."

Dawson suppressed a laugh, knowing full-well that Clancy and his sister-in-law did *not* get along. "I'm not sure what to say to that."

"Sergeant Major, if she moves in, I'm deploying with you. Hopefully I'll catch a bullet that puts me out of my misery."

Dawson laughed. "That's always an option. Or we could arrange a drone strike. Where's your sister-in-law live?"

"I'm afraid to tell you. If Niner finds out, he just might arrange it." Clancy sighed. "When I do retire, I'm going to miss this." He jerked a thumb over his shoulder. "Okay, let's head back. Tell the men to be ready to deploy in two hours. I want you in South Korea ASAP. I don't want to risk another team being assigned that'll take that kill shot without thinking." He turned slightly toward Dawson as he completed his U-turn. "But if the order is given, and you see no evidence that this is just another one of Kane's crazy plans, then take that shot. If he's betrayed his country, I don't care how good a friend he is. He dies."

Dawson's chest ached at the duty that lay ahead. "You can count on us, sir."

Even if it is the hardest kill I'll ever make.

Temporary Staff Quarters, CIA Headquarters

Langley, Virginia

Leroux flinched, reaching for his sleep mask as someone sat on the edge of his bed. He yanked it aside and relaxed as he recognized Sherrie's silhouette leaning over him.

"Sorry I woke you."

He did a self-assessment and found he felt much better. "How long have I been asleep?"

"Three hours."

"Oh shit! I told them to wake me in two."

"And I countermanded that order after talking to Sonya. The team is still working the problem, and she can handle things. The more rest you get now, the better."

"What's the status?"

"Bravo Team is in the air, and assets on the ground have interviewed the pilot that helped with the insertion. He had no idea what Dylan had planned, and was mad as hell when he opened up the door and jumped out. He depressurized the plane. Really messed things up and the pilot had to execute an emergency dive. He's got a bill for Kane if he ever decides to come back to this side of things."

"Hey, people are trying to sleep here!" protested someone at the far end of the bunkroom.

"Sorry," whispered Sherrie. She leaned in and gave Leroux a kiss. "Next time use your rank to get a private room. I'll make it worth your while." She patted his chest. "I'll let you get your rest."

Leroux shook his head. "No, I'm awake and I'm starving. Let's go to the caf' and talk." He rolled out of bed and Sherrie extended a hand, hauling him to his feet. They left the room, someone clapping as they exited, and made their way to the cafeteria where years ago he had bumped into his old high school buddy, rekindling the best friendship he had ever had.

And it crushed him.

He was working to save his friend, to prove there was something else going on, but he wasn't at the top of his game, and so far, all evidence suggested Kane was indeed defecting. Yet he couldn't be. He would have said something, even indirectly. Yes, he was dissatisfied with the direction the country was headed. He feared the polarization of the two sides could lead to civil war, or at the very least blood on the streets no matter who won the next election. They had all agreed that Western civilization was collapsing due to this polarization, but how was defecting to the most closed regime on the planet the solution?

It made no sense.

Sherrie grinned at him as he piled his tray with food, the smile spreading at the cash register as the rotund woman ringing it in gave him a look.

"Honey, if I ate like that, I'd be twice my size."

Sherrie patted him on the shoulder. "I help him burn it off."

The lady howled. "Oh, sugar, if I had a man like that at home, I'd be your size too."

Leroux blushed then tapped his phone to the reader before heading to a secluded table where they could talk. His stomach growled again in anticipation, confirming the need for the mountain of food, and he tucked into it as soon as his ass hit the plastic seat.

"Slow down, you'll just make yourself sick."

"*That* type of sick I can take."

Mushroom soup with broccoli, done.

Should have got two.

"So, I was right. I was called in because of what is happening with Dylan. Anyone who's worked with him in the past is being interviewed to see if there were any indicators we missed to suggest he was going to do this."

"And what did you say?"

BLT sandwich. Awesomesauce!

"I told them the truth, that he had never suggested any desire to defect, or ever questioned his loyalty to his country or the Agency."

"What about our discussions about society in general?"

"I didn't feel it was worth mentioning. We all feel the same way. If that were cause for concern, we'd all be getting fired."

Leroux grunted then took a swig of the 2% milk carton Sherrie had opened for him. "Yeah, I didn't say anything to the Chief either. There's something else going on here that we're not seeing, and I think the key is those messages."

"In what way?"

He cut into his meatloaf. "Who's sending them and how? And how do they know when to send them?"

Sherrie eyed him as he shoveled the oversized portion into his mouth. "Isn't that obvious? I mean, at least partially?"

Leroux stopped in mid-chew and stared at her. He covered his mouth. "What do you mean?"

"Well, you got the message through his secure network. That's not somebody on the outside sending messages, that's someone who has access to his private system. That has to be a small list of suspects."

"Perhaps, or he brought in someone new, or he automated it somehow."

"It still needs a trigger. It can't be a coincidence that the moment we identify it's him crossing the bridge, you and the Chief get messages. Someone had to have either told the person sending the messages for him, or triggered the automated system to send the message. Either way, the messages are being sent from somewhere."

Leroux scooped mashed potatoes into his mouth as he thought. Sherrie was right, of course. His mind had been a fog, but now was clearing. He felt dramatically better than just this morning, and his brain was functioning again. The key was the messages. If someone was sending them, or an automated routine was sending them, it didn't matter. The questions were, are there more, and what did they say? And what triggers would activate them? He put down his fork and finished his milk. "Could he be using his"—he lowered his voice and leaned in—"private ops center?"

Sherrie nodded. "That's what I was just thinking. Maybe we should pay it a visit."

Leroux picked up his fork, resuming his feeding frenzy. "I can't. I have to stay here. And besides, we have to keep this off the books." He paused. "What's your assignment?"

"Nothing at the moment. I'm still off. They just wanted to debrief me."

"Then why don't you and Fang check it out. It might be a dead-end, but you never know."

Sherrie smiled. "It would be nice to be doing something rather than just watching it all unfold. And it might help Fang deal with what she must be going through."

Leroux eyed the apple pie, his stomach begging him to stop. "That sounds like a plan. Do you remember the code to get in?"

"Yes. Let's hope he didn't change it."

"Well, if he did, then that might be a sign in itself."

Sherrie sighed. "Then let's hope he didn't. We need something to break our way soon, otherwise when Bravo Team lands, they'll be heading directly in to kill him, and there'll be nothing we can do to stop them."

Suddenly the pie lost its appeal.

Top Secret Nuclear Regulatory Commission Facility
Outside Seattle, Washington

"Good night, Dr. Burkett."

He gave the security guard a curt nod. "Good night." He pushed through the doors, heading into the parking lot. It was still half full, the entire building made up of eggheads working on the energy solutions of the future, some of which included those from the past. Everything from research into how to scrub the carbon out of fossil fuel emissions to mini-nuclear reactors that could power a small community, from solar paint to space mirrors that would focus the sun's energy onto massive solar farms, and so much more including geoengineering that personally terrified him.

It was one thing to take the carbon out of what man produced, it was a totally different thing to take it from the atmosphere, where mother nature expected it to be.

On paper, his job was to come up with the next generation of large-scale nuclear reactors. Unpopular with those who opposed anything but solar or wind, but the only real solution available to mankind for the next several decades. It was reliable, safe if done properly, and clean if the waste was stored properly. Science would eventually learn how to deal with the downsides. Abandoning the technology because you were afraid of it was foolish. Just look at Germany. A tsunami hits Fukushima in Japan and they abandon nuclear power in a country with almost no coastline and no history of major earthquakes.

And now they burn more coal.

So green.

When he was hired a couple of weeks ago, his supervisor told him it was his job to come up with the next generation of reactors that would settle the fears of the uneducated—a laudable goal.

Though he wouldn't be the one to accomplish that.

He fished the keys to his car out of his pocket and pressed the fob. The lights flashed on his Buick as the doors unlocked, and he relaxed slightly as yet another day of this existence ended. He couldn't wait for this to be over. He had been on countless assignments in his career, but this one was as boring as they got.

Nothing ever happened.

All day he simply dodged people, dodged questions, dodged meetings. He eyed the clock until he could escape at the end of the day, and just prayed that whatever happened, no one found out he was a fraud.

It was exhausting.

A van's engine roared to life as he passed, and several doors opened at once. He tensed slightly as he turned to see four masked men surge toward him, two with Glocks, the other two with Tasers. They fired and the prongs embedded into his chest and every muscle in his body clenched as he shook to the ground. His sphincter muscles released, and he thanked God he had gone to the bathroom just before he left, otherwise a figuratively shitty day would have ended as a literal one.

The Tasers stopped their torture but he continued to shake as they dragged him into the back of the van before it roared away. His mouth was taped and a hood was fitted over his head as duct tape bound his ankles and zip-ties cut into his wrists.

The entire operation took less than thirty seconds.

Pros.

At least it meant his days of faking his way through life were over.

Kane/Lee Residence, Fairfax Towers
Falls Church, Virginia

Lee Fang sat on the couch, staring at the news on mute, her knees drawn up to her chin, her fingers interlocked at her shins. She had been in this position for hours, ever since Sherrie had delivered the news. At first, she had refused to believe what she had been told, but the message Leroux had received was proof that it had happened.

Then she had moved on to his motivation. He had never mentioned anything to her about what he was planning, and they told each other everything. He had to be doing this against his will, and the message was something he had been coerced into sending. Yet Sherrie had described the video of his entry into North Korea, and it certainly didn't sound forced.

But appearances could be deceiving. She had been in the business, and there was a distinct possibility he still was being forced to do what he was doing. Someone could have blackmailed him into defecting. He might be doing it to save someone by sacrificing himself. He might be using this as an opportunity to gain access to something he might not otherwise be able to.

There were countless possibilities.

And she had to cling to them, because the alternative meant he was a traitor, something she refused to believe.

Her phone vibrated with a message and she picked it up, wiping her eyes dry on the back of her hand.

I'm sorry for what I've done. Hurting you was the most difficult thing I've ever done in my life. I hope one day you can forgive me.

She cried out in rage and sorrow as the phone clattered to the floor. The faint hope she had been clinging to was erased with a single message. He *had* defected. There was no doubt now. If this had all been some ruse, he never would have sent her a message. There was no need. And if he were being forced, they had a secret code worked out.

Give the cat a scratch for me.

Cats were the preferred code method in their world rather than dogs. Dogs were easy to confirm whether they existed. They had to be walked. Cats could live their entire lives within the four walls of an apartment and never make an appearance. And with some pet owners' irrational love for their animals, some beyond that of their human family members, it was believable that a reference to the animal could be made in a final message to a loved one.

She picked up the phone as her body shook, staring at the message, willing for another to come through with their secret code.

But none came.

She whipped the phone at the chair and it bounced off the back and smashed into the television, splintering the screen. A string of Chinese profanity erupted when a knock at the door silenced her.

Briefly.

"Leave me alone!" she screamed, then when a key hit the lock her heart leaped and she sprinted for the hallway. The door pushed open as she skidded to a halt then her shoulders collapsed as a concerned Sherrie entered rather than her beloved, traitorous boyfriend.

"Are you all right?" asked Sherrie as she closed the door then reached out for her. Fang collapsed into her arms, sobbing, her entire body shaking as she lost all will to live. She slid to the floor and Sherrie dropped with her, holding her the entire way, and they both sat there as they cried for what they had all lost.

Their innocence.

They had seen horrible things. They had done horrible things. But they had always had each other. The four of them were unbreakable. But now Kane had betrayed them all, and it meant that none of them could be counted on—something could turn any of them against the others if Kane could be.

"I have a mission if you feel up to it."

Fang sniffed and extricated herself from Sherrie's arms. "A mission?"

Sherrie rose and extended a hand. Fang took it and Sherrie hauled her to her feet, leading her back into the living room. Sherrie glanced at the broken TV and the phone lying on the floor in front of it. "Did it say something to piss you off?"

Fang giggled then bent over, picking up the phone. She handed it to Sherrie. "I got a message from Dylan."

Sherrie read it, frowning. "Yeah, there's been a lot of that going on. That's actually what our mission is about." She handed the phone back and the screen fell off. Fang tossed it on the table then picked up the remote control and turned off the equally useless TV. "How so?"

"Chris thinks the messages are all coming from Dylan's secure network. And the timing is too perfect. If he's in North Korea, then he shouldn't be able to trigger them—"

"Unless he already has their trust."

Sherrie shook her head. "No, I can't see that happening already. No matter how much he's told them, they wouldn't have trusted him quickly enough to send the message to Chris or the Chief."

"This could have been in the works for months for all we know. Kim Jong-un himself could have greeted him."

Again, Sherrie shook her head. "You're not thinking straight, and believe me, neither would I if I were in your shoes. He parachuted onto the bridge. If this were planned in cooperation with the North Koreans, they would have smuggled him into the country in a far less public way."

"Maybe they wanted it public."

"Then they would have brought him in by plane and had the press waiting in the jetway. No, this was as much a surprise to the North Koreans as it was to us."

Fang headed for the bedroom and Sherrie followed. "And what is this mission?"

Sherrie sat on the corner of the bed as Fang changed. "We're going to his ops center. Chris thinks the messages are getting sent from there, and he wants to know if there's some sort of trigger. We might have a mole in the Agency controlling it, and if there's a mole, that's someone we can interrogate."

"If we can find him."

"Oh, we'll find him. The Chief is pissed, and he wants to get to the bottom of this."

Fang finished then faced Sherrie, holding her arms wide. "Well?"

"If looks could kill…"

Fang laughed then sighed. "I'm an emotional wreck." She headed to the closet and unlocked the gun locker it contained. She pulled out a Glock and a few spare mags, along with several small knives, tucking them into discreet locations. She secured the locker and closed the closet doors. "Let's get the hell out of here so I can kill something."

Sherrie grinned. "I doubt we're killing anything, but when we get there, feel free to fire off a few rounds at a tree or something."

Fang tucked the gun away. "I'm driving."

"No way in hell. You'll get us both killed in your state."

Fang huffed.

"But I'll tell you what. When we get there, you can take point."

Fang smiled. "Deal."

Over US Airspace

"Bullshit! Complete and utter bullshit! Of all the bullshit I've heard in my career, that is the bullshittiest of them all!"

Atlas eyed Niner. "Tell us how you really feel, little man."

Niner turned on him. "What, you believe this bullshit?"

"Not for a second."

"Then what the hell?"

Atlas shrugged. "I enjoy pushing your buttons?" The big man turned to Dawson who was briefing them from the front of the plane. "He's right, BD. This is bullshit."

Dawson agreed. "You'll get no argument from me, Sergeant. I said as much to the colonel, who also thinks it's bullshit. But nonetheless, Kane crossed the border into North Korea yesterday, and has sent several messages to key personnel at the CIA confirming what they suspect—Dylan Kane has defected willingly to North Korea."

Spock cocked an eyebrow. "Willingly? Are we sure about that?"

Dawson threw up his hands. "None of the messages I've been briefed on have given any indication he was forced into this. According to Langley, everything so far indicates he has willingly defected to North Korea. Nobody knew he was planning it, including his friends."

"Could they be lying?"

Dawson shrugged. "Anything's possible, and if that's the case, then we've got a bigger problem than just one asset defecting. We have people deep within the CIA who covered for him, and are still covering for him."

Sergeant Eugene "Jagger" Thomas pursed his massive lips. "And one of them is Control on this mission?"

"Yes."

"Can we trust him?" asked Sergeant Gerry "Jimmy Olsen" Hudson.

"Do we have a choice?" Dawson held up a hand, cutting off any response. "Listen, I find it impossible to believe that Leroux and the others knew he was going to do this. Let's assume he has actually defected. If he told his girlfriend or Leroux, or anyone else in that group, they would have tried to convince him not to. And when they failed, they would have reported him so that they could save him from himself."

Niner glanced at Atlas. "I'd turn you in in a heartbeat."

Atlas grunted. "I'd just shoot you in the head then tell BD why."

"That's because I love you and want to save you. You just want to hurt me."

"If I wanted to hurt you, I'd shoot you in the ass."

Dawson gave them both a look. "Done?"

Niner grinned. "I wouldn't count on it."

"As I was saying, they'd turn him in to save him. Nobody did. This came completely out of the blue, which tells me that he didn't tell any of them, because he knew they would try and stop him."

Spock shifted in his seat. "Or, this *is* all bullshit, and he hasn't really defected at all, so there was no need to tell them anything."

Jagger frowned. "I thought of that too, but if he weren't defecting, then wouldn't he want his closest friends to know so they could help him? I mean, how the hell does he plan to escape now that he's delivered himself into their hands?"

Dawson shook his head. "If there's a mole inside the CIA, then he might not want any of his friends knowing anything. If they knew what he was going to do, they might not react the way they should. That could blow his cover."

Atlas scratched at his massive bicep. "So, basically what you're saying is we have no damned clue what's going on, just that the brass is convinced he has defected, and they want us to go in and take him out before he spills too many state secrets."

"Basically."

"Well, that sucks."

"No shit," agreed Niner. He leaned forward. "I don't know about the rest of you, but I'm not sure I can take the shot. He's a friend. A comrade. Hell, he's saved my life. What if we're wrong? What if Langley is wrong? What if he's there for a damned good reason, and we go in and kill him because we don't have all the intel?"

Dawson agreed with his friend but had to nip this talk in the bud. "Listen, I understand how you're feeling. I'm sure we all feel the same way. But that's why we're being sent in. We won't blindly take the shot without thinking. We're being sent in *because* we have those doubts. We'll go in, assess the situation, and if ordered, take the shot unless we observe something that is out of character for him. We're going in because *we* know him. It is essential that we pay attention to everything we see. His body language, anything we overhear, anything we see him do that doesn't fit with what we know about him."

Niner grunted. "I think defecting to Nutbar Land doesn't fit with what we know about him."

"Agreed. But remember, if we're lucky enough to get our eyes on him, he won't know it. He's going to be assuming that a hit squad has been sent to take him out, and he specifically challenged his own Chief to send the best. He knows someone like us could be watching at any time. If he's up to something, he'll give us a signal if he can."

Atlas disagreed. "Wishful thinking, BD. If he's actually defected, he's going to know everything you just said, and if he wants to survive, he's going to give us that signal so we don't shoot him."

Niner growled. "We're damned if we do, damned if we don't. How the hell are we going to know if he's just playing us, or if he really is still on our side?"

Spock frowned. "There's no way to know except to go with our gut."

Jagger closed his eyes. "Or we err on the side of caution and take him out the first chance we get."

The uncertainty on his team's faces was evident, and Dawson set their minds at ease. Somewhat. "If any shot is to be taken, I'll give the order. This will be my call. Understood?"

A string of acknowledgments responded and he could see the thanks in many of their eyes. One of them might still have to kill a friend, but if that friend had gone to the dark side, he was never the man they knew, and deserved whatever happened to him.

And a bullet to the head might just be merciful should the North Koreans tire of their new friend.

Over the Pacific Ocean
International Airspace

Major Choe Yong-dae stared at their prisoner, handcuffed to his seat near the rear of the charter jet. Abducting him had been easy, as easy as described. Getting away with it was the more difficult matter. The facility Dr. Burkett worked at undoubtedly had impressive internal security, but once through the doors, it was just any other office building.

The Americans didn't want its enemies knowing the type of work going on in the sleepy suburban neighborhood adjacent to a major metropolis. This was one of their facilities that acknowledged the cream of the crop, the best and brightest, no longer wanted to be taken to the middle of nowhere to live for years while they toiled away on top-secret projects for their government.

Today's patriot wanted to drive to work from their luxurious home, do their job, then return home, with all the amenities living close to a city provided.

Decadence.

It was what would ultimately destroy America and leave countries like Choe's victorious in the end.

The abduction had been easy, and once clear of the building, a known dead zone was used to transfer their prisoner to another vehicle, and they were soon on their charter heading over the Pacific. The Americans couldn't touch them now, even if they tracked them. The only option would be to shoot them down, in international airspace, and lose their scientist.

The question was whether they would rather him dead than in enemy hands. He was betting the weak-kneed leadership in Washington would do nothing.

Stationed in America as a covert operative for the North Korean people, he was privy to all their news and propaganda. He always found it hilarious how the Americans and the West in general responded to his country's nuclear program. With each test of a new bomb, with each firing of a new missile, his country grew closer and closer to total security. Once the technology was perfected, their borders would be secure. No one could touch them once his country could detonate a warhead over any city on the planet.

It was just a matter of time, and as long as the West continued to simply protest rather than act, his country would win in the end.

And apparently, this man they now had in custody could help them achieve that.

Though he appeared awfully young.

One of his men rose from interrogating the prisoner and joined him at the front of the plane. No names were used, only ranks. Should something go wrong, the less one knew about other sleepers stationed in America, the better.

"Well?"

The captain shrugged. "I asked him the questions Command provided, and he seemed to answer correctly, though I'll be honest with you, sir, this stuff is way over my head."

"We'll let Command decide if he was worth all this." Choe pursed his lips, eying the prisoner who appeared relatively calm, staring out the window of the plane rather than at his captors. "How old do you think he is?"

"Thirty-ish? Apparently he's some genius. Graduated college before he was eighteen. Has multiple advanced degrees. Everything checks out so far with what Command provided. I'm sure he's our guy. He matches the photo we were sent, and like I said, seems to know his stuff."

Choe checked his watch. "We'll be on the ground in eleven hours. Command will confirm things then."

"Assuming the Americans don't shoot us down first."

Choe grunted. "If he's that important, they would never have let him be out on his own."

The captain eyed him. "Do you think this was a waste of time?"

"I hope not. If he can help with our nuclear program, he could be the key to securing our country's future."

"These Imperial Dogs won't want that. I still think they just might try to shoot us down."

"If they do, then another team will kidnap another scientist and use another means of escape. No matter what happens, the Dear Leader will be victorious."

Ministry of State Security Headquarters

Pyongyang, North Korea

"Is this him?" Major Pak held out the photo of the prisoner the team had taken outside Seattle, and Kane nodded.

"Yup, that's him. My God, I forgot how young he is. He's like my age."

Pak sat across from the American. "Yes, he is. It has raised many questions at Command. How can someone so young bring us the nuclear power that your government would deny our citizens?"

Kane shrugged. "You guys get Doogie Howser here?"

Pak eyed him. "What?"

"Never mind. Certainly you have child geniuses here like we do back home?"

Pak gave a curt nod. "Of course."

"Well, imagine if one of them were able to attend the best schools the world had to offer, and had an aptitude for the sciences. He or she could be your savior. Unfortunately for you, those children can't get into those schools, and that knowledge is denied to your people. It's like at SpaceX. They were accused of being discriminatory because the vast majority of their workforce was American, and of course the bandwagon jumpers who never let facts get in the way piled on, accusing them of being racist. The reality is that rocket technology is considered military weaponry, so the security clearances are a bitch if you're not a US citizen. Imagine if a North Korean wanted to work at SpaceX. It would never be allowed to happen, no matter how gifted your prodigy was. My guy, however, is an American citizen, which means he can pass all the security clearances, get the best education, get the best training, and by the time he's my age, have more experience than someone twice his age, and because of his security clearance, be exposed to more knowledge and secrets than you can possibly imagine just because of where he was born."

"America."

"Land of the free, home of the brave."

"You sound as if you still admire it."

"I do. Not everything about my country is bad, but I fear it has a reckoning coming, and the sooner it comes, the better. Think of the Dark Ages. Eight hundred years of progress wasted. We'd be colonizing other planets by now, traveling the stars, if we hadn't wasted so much time. The same with back home. As long as we're at each other's throats, we'll never move forward. Better to get the killing started now. We might lose a decade or two, but eventually it will be over, and my country can move forward, united."

"At which time you'll want to return home."

Kane shrugged. "Perhaps. By then anything of use that I know will have long expired, and your country, thanks to the help I will provide you over the coming months and years, will have progressed rapidly. You'll have nuclear power to keep the lights on, nuclear weapons that can reach anywhere in the world to protect your borders, and if you let me, I'll get you scientists that can increase your productivity, your food supply, and anything else you need. North Korea will be a modern state that hasn't had to cave into this democracy nonsense where every uninformed idiot gets a vote."

Pak regarded the man. He wanted to believe him. He wanted to trust him as much as you could ever trust a man who would betray his own country, yet he couldn't. This was all simply too good to be true. This man just shows up with no announcement, no preliminary contact, no informal outreach to see if his overtures would be accepted? This wasn't how it was done.

His government was approached all the time by people interested in defecting, but the vast majority of the time, after some initial vetting, they were found to be crackpots. Those that weren't, more often than not, were of no use to his country. They were failed citizens of their own state that wanted to relocate to another they believed would provide them with everything. While the communist state did provide, it still expected the citizen to work, to contribute positively to the collective.

Freeloaders were not welcome, no matter what country they came from.

But this man was different. He appeared to be the real thing. What little they had found out about this Dr. Burkett matched Kane's story. His superiors had expressed concern there wasn't much information out there on this so-called prodigy, but that wasn't a concern to him. The American government would have done everything it could to scrub its prized asset from the Internet. According to the team that had extracted him, he had correctly answered all the questions that North Korea's top nuclear scientists had come up with on short notice, though as the commander had said, none of his men understood the questions asked and certainly couldn't comprehend the answers. Pak had a feeling the assessment of the accuracy of the responses was more based on the confidence in which they were delivered by Burkett. A recording of the Q and A session had been made and would be reviewed by their scientists to confirm the accuracy.

If Kane were telling the truth then his defection could indeed be one of the most damaging in American history, for there was no way to protect against the havoc he could unleash on his abandoned homeland. Most defectors came with specific knowledge. An intelligence asset might know the names and locations of spies or handlers or some other thing temporarily valuable, but Kane had come to them with a unique proposition—identifying sources of knowledge in the scientific community that could prove valuable for decades to come.

If Burkett was who he appeared to be, the North Korean nuclear power program faltering for sixty years might finally bear fruit, something that would benefit his country for generations, far more than identifying a spy in their midst that could be replaced the next day. Knowledge was key, and Kane just might bring his country back from the brink.

He tapped his pen on the pad of paper in front of him. "We need an expert in ICBM rocketry, including submarine-launched. We want to be able to hit any target in the world should it become necessary."

Kane smiled. "Those are actually two different areas of expertise and I know people in both."

"And their names are?"

Kane shook his head. "No, you get one for free. When Burkett checks out and we come to an agreement, then I'll give you as many as you want. But right now, I'm still in a prison cell with none of what I've asked for."

Pak frowned, disappointed in the answer despite the fact it wasn't unexpected. He would do the same if he were in Kane's position. "Very well. Dr. Burkett should be here within the next half day. Once he's been vetted, and assuming all goes well, I'm sure we'll be able to come to some sort of agreement."

"I'm sure we can. However, in the meantime, would it be possible to have me in better quarters? You could throw as many guards on me as you want, and a tracking device if you feel it's necessary. But I'd just like to be in a room where the walls aren't crumbling concrete, the floor isn't wet, and the mattress isn't something from the war."

Pak chuckled. "I'll see what I can arrange."

Kane extended a hand and Pak shook it. "Thank you very much, Major. It's truly appreciated. I hope that one day you and I will call each other friend."

Pak rose and headed for the door. "I'm afraid, Mr. Kane, that as soon as you have been cleared, our time together will be finished and you will never see me again, unless you betray your new home."

Kane's shoulders sagged slightly. "Am I to have any friends here?"

"In time, I'm sure, but expect to be alone for a while. You'll find it takes time for my people to trust someone who believes so differently from them."

"I understand. Then perhaps part of the bargain will have to be paid, shall we say, companionship?"

Pak peered at him. "I'm afraid I don't understand."

"Women, Major. Prostitutes, hookers, escorts, whatever you call them here. Paid companionship."

"We don't have that in North Korea."

"I believe that's the first lie you've told me, Major. I haven't lied to you yet, so I highly suggest you save the lies for when they really matter. You have women trained for this, just like we do. I'm looking for someone to be my live-in girlfriend. Beautiful, of course, willing, but also someone to just talk to so I don't have to spend the days and nights alone."

Pak eyed the man. It was one of the most frequent demands made by people in this position. They assumed that their new host country would be so grateful, they'd be willing to throw their women at them in thanks. It was rarely granted, and as most defectors the world over eventually discovered, their lives as they knew it were over and would quite often be spent alone. Yet this was an opportunity to introduce a spy into Kane's home environment, where he might slip up and say something he shouldn't, that might reveal any hidden truths. And Kane was right. They did have women trained for this, women they would send into foreign countries to seduce men and women of power and catch them on camera in compromising positions.

Perhaps the request wasn't so unreasonable after all.

He opened the door. "I'll see what can be arranged."

Kane smiled but held up a finger. "Just remember, if I don't like her, you have to get me a new one and keep getting me new ones until I'm satisfied."

Pak closed the door, his skin crawling at the thought that one of his female comrades would be forced to have sex with this man, perhaps for years to come. Yet if she kept him happy and he kept providing the names of those they would need, she would be recognized as a hero of the homeland and perhaps even the mother of its future.

Though it still disgusted him.

Director Morrison's Office, CIA Headquarters

Langley, Virginia

Leroux entered Morrison's office, and before he could take a seat in front of the desk, the Chief held up his cellphone, a message displayed. Leroux stepped closer to the desk and bent over, peering at the screen.

Burkett was just the first of many to come. You better kill me soon.

Leroux stepped back and sat. "Who the hell is Burkett?"

Morrison shook his head. "No idea, but I want you to find out. I'm more curious about the rest of the message. It's like he's taunting us to kill him and to kill him quickly. Could he be suicidal?"

Leroux threw his hands up. "He certainly gave no indication to any of us that he was unhappy. Hell, I've never seen him happier since he's been with Fang. He's got his self-destructive behavior under control, he's finally faced the nightmare that's been haunting him, and for the first time in his life, he's actually in love."

Morrison tossed his cellphone on the desk then leaned back. "So, no indication whatsoever?"

"None. I'll have Sherrie talk to Fang, though. If anyone would know, it would be her. Certainly Sherrie and I haven't noticed anything."

"I'm having Thorn brought in. There are some things that operatives share with their handlers that they share with no one else."

"Have you spoken to her yet?"

Morrison shook his head. "No. In fact, she doesn't know she's coming in."

Leroux cocked an eyebrow. "What do you mean?"

"I mean, if she's in on it, I don't want to give her any opportunity to destroy evidence."

"You mean—"

"I mean, she's being taken in against her will."

"Are you bringing her here?"

"No, there's no time for that. She'll be taken to a secure facility in Europe where a trusted asset will interview her."

"Who's the asset?"

"Someone we've worked with before, someone who knows both her and Kane. Someone I can trust to keep their mouth shut about what's going on." Morrison checked his watch. "Someone who should be paying her a visit right about now."

Thorn Residence

Wiesingerstraße, Vienna, Austria

Beverly Thorn sipped her Turkish coffee. She had perfected the proper preparation method years ago, resulting in an always satisfying brew, yet it was never as exquisite as the real thing in the Grand Bazaar of Istanbul—the Turks just seemed to have some secret ingredient that she couldn't replicate in her apartment in Vienna. Despite years of attempting to figure out what was missing, she had never succeeded, and was now convinced that it wasn't an ingredient or a method at all, but merely the locale. Baguettes were always better in Paris, beignets always better in New Orleans, and barbecue always better in Texas.

Turkish coffee was always better in Turkey, and fortunately for her, her business took her there frequently. It was the intersection of East and West, bordering on so many of the enemies she dealt with on a daily basis, yet with the safety of a NATO country. Turkey was a perfect meeting spot for many of the operations officers and various other assets she managed for the CIA, men and women she had known for years, some for decades, many she thought of as her children.

An uncustomary knock at her door had her briefly tensing. She received few unexpected guests. Whoever was on the other side of that door likely had something to do with the message she had received minutes ago from one of her dearest operatives. She was just surprised they were here so quickly.

She sighed and rose then headed for the door. She didn't bother peering through the peephole. If whoever was on the other side of that door wanted her dead, she'd be dead. She unlocked then opened it, and smiled at the man standing in the hallway. "Quentin Jackson. I didn't think I'd ever see you again."

Jackson smiled warmly at her and bowed his head. "It's great to see you again, Ms. Thorn, especially looking so well."

She stepped aside and beckoned him in. "Yes, I suppose the last time you saw me I wasn't in the best of condition."

"No, you weren't."

"I just made coffee," she said as she closed the door. "Do you have time?"

"Of course."

Jackson sat at the kitchen table where she had been relaxing moments ago. She poured him a cup and topped up her own before sitting across from him. She logged into her phone and brought up the message she had received, then pushed it across to her guest. "I assume you're here because of this?"

Jackson leaned forward and read the message. "I'm sorry if what I've done causes you any problems. You were always good to me, and this has nothing to do with you." He sat back. "When did you receive it?"

"Barely ten minutes ago."

"When was the last time you heard from him?"

Thorn shook her head and tapped the table beside the phone. "First, I want you to explain this."

Jackson leaned back and folded his arms. "You don't know?"

"If I knew, I wouldn't be asking. What's going on?"

He eyed her for a moment. "You really don't know, do you?"

"I think we've established that. What's going on with my asset?"

"He's defected to North Korea."

She had prepared herself for any number of answers, but never in a million years would she have come up with the one she had just been given. Kane defecting to North Korea? It made no sense and there was no way it was true. If he were to defect to an enemy, which she couldn't imagine him ever doing, he would go to China. At least there he could have a good life, and he did have a penchant for their women. He might even swing a deal to have Fang forgiven for her past transgressions so she could return to her homeland. But North Korea? It was insane. The country was a hellhole. Even the elite suffered, and there was nothing the North Koreans could do to help Fang. He would live a lonely, meager life there. But all of that was irrelevant.

There was no way Dylan Kane had defected.

"Bullshit," she finally replied.

Jackson grunted. "That appears to be the prevailing opinion."

"What proof do you have?"

"Besides all kinds of key people receiving messages similar to what you received? We have him on video parachuting onto the Bridge of No Return in the Joint Security Area, then walking willingly onto their side of the border and exchanging pleasantries. This happened. He is there in their custody, and every indication is he went there willingly. Hell, the last briefing I got from the Chief just before I came said Kane challenged him to send the best we've got to kill him."

Thorn's eyes narrowed. Kane was cocky. It was one of the things that made him a great operative, but he knew how and when to turn it off. Was he show-boating because he didn't think he could be touched now that he was under the protection of the North Koreans? Or did he have a death wish? Was this all an elaborate ploy to get himself killed?

"Has he given any indications that he's been upset with anything? Depressed, suicidal?"

Thorn shook her head. "No, otherwise I would have pulled him from the roster. You can't have an asset like that in the field."

"So, he gave you no indication he was going through anything."

Thorn shook her head. "Nothing whatsoever, which is why I think this is bullshit. What does the Chief have planned for him?"

"I'm not privy to that, but I would assume a team is being sent in to either extract him or eliminate him."

Thorn bit her lip. "They won't risk personnel trying to extract him. Besides, it could create an international incident."

"A single shot to the head from a safe distance then?"

"That's how I'd do it." She sighed, her heart aching. The young man was like a son to her. She had been his handler for years, and while she worried about him every time she sent him out on a mission and prepared herself for the possibility he might not be coming back, this was something entirely different. He had betrayed his country and would be killed for it, quite likely by someone he knew.

And yet she didn't believe it for a second.

"We need to find out what's really going on, before that shot's taken."

"I'm sure Langley's working on it, but I have a team waiting to go through all of your stuff."

She chuckled. "My dear, the moment I received that message, I knew something was wrong, so I initiated standard protocol. All my data has been wiped. All I kept was the message."

Jackson cursed. "Why would you do that?"

"Because if my asset was compromised, he could have given me up under torture then a team could have been sent here and gained access to all my data. That could have compromised all of the assets I manage."

Jackson sighed. "I suppose you're right. So, you have nothing?"

"Just the message."

"Do you mind if my team does its sweep regardless?"

She flicked her wrist. "Knock yourself out. I followed my standard procedure, you have to follow yours. But tell the Chief this, I don't believe for one moment that Dylan Kane has defected to North Korea."

Jackson rose from the table and headed for the door. "Neither do I."

Operations Center 2, CIA Headquarters

Langley, Virginia

Leroux entered the operations center and headed immediately for Tong's station. "Anything yet on that Burkett?"

"Yes. We just got a report of a kidnapping outside of Seattle. One Dr. Leonard Burkett was abducted from the parking lot of a top-secret Nuclear Regulatory Commission facility by unknown individuals in a van."

Leroux whistled. "Holy shit. Who is he?"

"According to the bio that was attached to the report, he's some sort of genius nuclear physicist. Way ahead of his time. This guy is like Sheldon Cooper smart."

"Huh. Well, if the message Dylan sent the Chief is any indication, it was the North Koreans that nabbed him. Any word on the investigation?"

"It happened less than an hour ago. They found the vehicle that was used during the abduction in a camera dead zone, and they managed to figure out what vehicle they switched into. It was found at a charter airport nearby."

"And let me guess, where the occupants boarded a private jet that was already waiting for them?"

Tong grinned. "It's like you've seen this before."

Leroux rolled his eyes then sat at his station. "A few times, I'm sure. Okay, where's the plane now?"

"Unfortunately, it's already in international airspace. We can't touch it."

"Where's it going?"

"The flight plan that was filed shows they are heading to Beijing, but it would be nothing for them to change course at the last minute and head into North Korea."

Leroux scratched his chin. "It'll be interesting to see what they do."

"Why's that?" asked Child, spinning yet again.

"Well, Dylan's told us that it's the North Koreans that have done this, which means he doesn't care that we know. If they land in China, then that means they're trying to hide their involvement. If they land in North Korea, then they're not."

Child dropped his foot, killing his spin. "So, what does that tell us?"

Leroux turned in his chair to face their youngest analyst. "It tells us a lot. If Kane's told us that he's behind this with the North Koreans, and the North Koreans land in China, then that means they don't know he's told us. That means he's up to something that he doesn't want them to know about. But if they land in North Korea, then he's working lockstep with them." He turned to Tong as a thought occurred to him. "Check the timing of that message the Chief received about Burkett against when that private jet crossed into international airspace."

Tong worked her keyboard and cursed.

"Well?"

"Less than five minutes after they crossed into international airspace."

Leroux leaned back, clasping his hands behind his head. "There's no way in hell he's sending the messages. There's no way those on the plane could get word back to their people, then for it to make its way down the chain to Dylan, then for him to send that message."

Tong cleared her throat. "There is *one* way."

Leroux regarded her. "What?"

"That he *is* actually working for them. He could be sitting in their control center right now, privy to the information as it comes in."

Leroux frowned. She was right. He was blinded by his bias that his friend was innocent, that he was doing this for some purpose that would all become clear. But all of his assumptions were worthless if Kane were indeed guilty. He turned to Marc Therrien. "Marc, I want you to talk to a few of the staff doctors. See if there are any medical conditions that might explain what's happened to him, something that could trigger a personality change."

"Like a stroke?"

"Or anything that could explain him being perfectly fine one moment then working for the other side the next."

"You got it, boss. I assume you want me to keep this on the down-low?"

"Yes."

Therrien left the operations center and Tong lowered her voice as she leaned closer. "Do you really think it could be something like that?"

Leroux sighed, shaking his head. "I doubt it, but I'm grasping at straws here." He closed his eyes. "When will they have to change course if they're going to land in North Korea?"

"About ten hours from now."

"Then I guess we wait."

And pray that flight goes to China.

En route to Bethesda, Maryland

Sherrie drove. There was no way in hell she was letting Fang behind the wheel in her current state of mind. The drive had been a mix of emotions for both of them. She obviously wasn't as close with Kane as Fang was, but she still considered him one of her best friends. They were in the same business, had shed blood together, had been on ops together, and had saved each other's lives. There was nothing she wouldn't do for him as a fellow operative and as a friend. She could only imagine what Leroux must be going through. Kane was Leroux's only friend and they were like brothers. Polar opposites in many ways, but still the best of friends. If Kane turned out to be a traitor, it would devastate her boyfriend and he might never trust anyone again.

Yet his pain was nothing compared to what Fang was going through. This was the love of her life betraying not only his country, but her as well. And she was utterly alone. Outside of this close-knit group, all of her family, friends, and colleagues back in China knew her only as a traitor, and she had to leave them thinking that. Any attempt to contact them could put their lives at risk.

But Fang had been happy for years now that she and Kane were together. She was making a new life for herself and seemed content. What she would do if she lost her boyfriend, especially in this way, Sherrie had no idea.

"I'll have to join him."

Sherrie's eyebrows shot up. "Excuse me?"

"If he's really defected, I'll have to join him."

"Are you nuts? We're talking about North Korea here."

Fang shrugged. "If he's done it, he's done it for a good reason, and maybe I can understand that reasoning if I get a chance to talk to him in person. And I know we can be happy together anywhere."

Sherrie sighed. "You're not thinking straight. You know damn well the moment they realize who you are, they're handing you over to China to win brownie points."

"They wouldn't dare, not if they wanted Dylan to continue cooperating."

"That's assuming he knows you even arrived in North Korea."

Fang punched the dash, a string of curses in Mandarin erupting. "I feel so helpless!"

Sherrie reached over and took her friend's hand, giving it a squeeze. "We all do, but hopefully once we get to the operations center we'll know more."

Fang peered about, as if noticing their surroundings for the first time. "How much longer?"

Sherrie glanced at the trip odometer, knowing how long their journey should take. "Less than ten minutes."

Fang checked her Glock. "Remember, I'm going in first."

Sherrie frowned. "Do you really think that's a good idea? You could kill our only witness."

"If it was meant to be, it was meant to be."

Kane's off-the-books Operations Center

Outside Bethesda, Maryland

He had been entirely alone for four days since Kane had dropped him off at this compact but extremely capable operations center. Built into two shipping containers nestled among a sea of containers and trailers in the middle of nowhere, it had been his home for what felt like an eternity. He wasn't privy to where they actually were, though he was quite certain they were still in Maryland based upon the length of the drive and the number of twists and turns it took to get here.

He was supposed to be safe, but he wasn't so sure. Something very strange was going on. His instructions had been simple. Every time the system received a message with a code embedded, he would send a corresponding message. The system was already programmed with the text of the message and the destination, none of which he was privy to. He was merely there to make sure the proper message was sent at the proper time. Everything else was automated. He was certain if he had been given the chance, he could have automated the process entirely so that he wouldn't even be needed.

But whenever Dylan Kane called, he answered and did what was wanted because the payday was always good. But he was bored stiff, and he had no idea how much longer he'd be here. The facility wasn't luxurious, but it was well equipped. He had a comfortable bed, a good bathroom, and plenty of food and water. He could stay here for months, though he had no desire to despite being paid four figures a day just to be here. And despite what some people thought, he did have a life of his own, and he had no desire to spend any more time here than he needed to.

Unfortunately, Kane had given no indication as to how long he'd need to be here, but he had a sense it wasn't too much longer. He had become bored, so had hacked the system and found there were only six more messages in the queue waiting to be sent. At the rate he'd been sending them over the past two days, he got the sense that whatever was going on, his involvement could be coming to an end within the next 24 hours. Which begged the question, how the hell was he getting home? He had no idea where he was. He had no car.

He cursed aloud.

He hadn't really thought this through. He had just trusted the man, yet there was no reason to believe that after the last message was sent, Kane wouldn't be coming through the hidden door just down the corridor.

A red light blinked rapidly to his left, followed by a buzzing sound. He gulped. It was the perimeter alarm indicating someone was outside.

He turned toward the wall of monitors behind him, each showing different security camera angles. And he nearly fainted as two shadowy figures crept along the outside wall, both with handguns. His bladder let go, and he thanked God he had just gone to the bathroom, giving him time to squeeze and hold without a mess.

This wasn't part of the bargain. Nobody had said anything about holding out against attackers. The two figures made their way around to where the door was hidden, and his eyes shot wide when one of them slid aside the secret panel hiding the keypad.

How the hell do they know where that is?

They tried the code several times, but the system indicated it was incorrect. Whoever they were knew exactly where he was located and where the panel was, but their intel was obviously incomplete or not entirely accurate, since whatever code they thought was in use wasn't. It would keep them out for now, but he was at a loss as to what to do should they persist. It wasn't like he could call the police, and Kane had specifically told him there would be no way to reach him during the mission.

He was on his own.

One of them glanced up at the camera, yet another thing that they shouldn't have known where it was, and he gasped. He leaped from his seat and rushed down the corridor then unlocked the door and threw it open. "What are you two doing here?"

Sherrie's jaw dropped and Fang's weapon pressed against his neck. "I think the better question is, what are *you* doing here?"

But the question was only half heard as Tommy Granger fainted and collapsed to the floor.

Kane's off-the-books Operations Center

Outside Bethesda, Maryland

Fang paced back and forth impatiently as Sherrie searched the med kit. Tommy lay on one of the beds, still unconscious, but alive. If she hadn't known him, she likely would have put a bullet through his skull, but Tommy Granger was just a kid, maybe mid-twenties. He was a computer genius that had helped them out on multiple occasions, and as innocent as they came—there was no way in hell he was working for the North Koreans, though perhaps he was unwittingly. Most people were naïve when it came to how the world really worked.

"Found it!" Sherrie triumphantly held up a capsule of smelling salts. She snapped the vial and waved the pungent ammonia in front of Tommy's nose. He winced then batted it away before his eyes fluttered open. He scrambled into the corner as his eyes focused. He finally recognized them and his shoulders slumped as he exhaled loudly.

"Oh, thank God it's you! You have no idea how bored I've been." He eyed them. "But what are you doing here? He said I'd be alone the entire time."

Fang surged forward, ready to wring more answers out of him, but Sherrie blocked her with an arm. Fang turned away and instead listened as her eyes continued the evaluation of their surroundings. Judging by the mess, Tommy had been here for days. Clothes were strewn about, as were food wrappers and containers. The man was a pig.

"Who said you'd be alone?" asked Sherrie.

"Dylan. Who else?"

Fang resisted the urge to ask just what the hell was going on.

"Dylan brought you here?"

"Yes. Four days ago."

Fang glanced over her shoulder at Sherrie, and they exchanged a puzzled look. "Four days ago? And what have you been doing since?"

"Just monitoring communications. Every time the system gets a message with a code in it, I send the corresponding coded message."

Sherrie cursed. "So that's how he's been doing it."

"What do you mean? Do you know what's going on?"

Fang turned. "Did he tell you why he did it?"

Tommy looked at Fang. "I'm sorry. Did what?"

Sherrie explained. "Tommy, as far as the world knows, Dylan defected to North Korea two days ago."

Tommy gasped. "Bullshit!"

"That's what we think, too. But those messages you've been sending, each one of them confirms what he's done, and we've got footage of him walking across the border. And one of those messages you sent claims credit for the kidnapping of a top-secret scientist who was abducted earlier this evening."

"Holy shit!" exclaimed Tommy as he paled. "Was anybody hurt?" he asked, his voice barely a whisper.

"Not during the kidnapping, but we don't know the current status of the scientist."

"Who was he?"

"Nobody you would have ever heard of, I'm sure. Apparently, he's some genius physicist that specializes in nuclear power."

Tommy, already a pasty white on a good day, paled even further. "So, if the North Koreans have taken him—"

"Then they might be able to get their nuclear power program up and running, which will give them a stable power supply, and with the nuclear waste, it would generate an inexhaustible supply of dirty bomb material."

Fang pulled at her hair. "Not to mention the fact that you could have another possible Chernobyl sitting in the hands of a completely incompetent regime that would never ask for help, no matter how desperate the situation was. Remember, when the Russians were denying there was a problem, Chernobyl was in full meltdown and had the potential to irradiate all of Europe, killing hundreds of millions of people."

Tommy's head dropped between his knees, his hands dangling loosely at his sides. "And I helped do this."

Sherrie gave his shoulder a squeeze. "You didn't know. You were just following the orders of someone you trusted. If it had been me, I would have been sending the messages as well."

Tommy grunted. "Yeah, but it wasn't you, was it?" He inhaled loudly then pushed to his feet. "What do we do now?"

"We need to find out what messages have been sent and what messages are still waiting."

Tommy glanced at Fang. "Don't we know what's been sent?"

She shook her head. "No. We know some of what's been sent, but there could be others that we're not aware of. There could be others involved that are helping him out. Do you think you can hack his system?"

"I already did. That's why I know there are six more messages to be sent."

"Have you read them?" asked Sherrie, excited.

He shook his head. "No, they're encrypted."

"Do you think you could break the encryption?"

"Not a hope in hell, if I know him. Maybe if I had a supercomputer. But I should be able to tell you where they're going to be sent."

Fang's eyes narrowed. "You mean he didn't encrypt the phone numbers?"

Tommy grinned and headed toward the operations center. "Oh, he encrypted them, but all we need to do is match up who got what messages when. And since we know those numbers, we can break the encryption key with ease. Remember, each digit of a phone number only has ten possibilities." He sat in front of one of the terminals. "Did either of you get a message?"

Fang nodded. "I did."

"Do you have the exact time it was sent?"

She shook her head. "I don't have the phone with me."

Tommy spun in his chair, his eyes wide. "You don't have the phone with you? Why not?"

Fang said nothing but Sherrie grinned. "Because she put it through her television set."

Tommy stared at them blankly for a moment. "Oh, okay. Did *you* get a message?"

Sherrie shook her head. "No, but Chris did and so did the Chief."

"Then we just need to find out when they got their messages. And Fang, if you loosely remember when you received yours, that should be enough."

Sherrie pulled out her phone and dialed Leroux as Fang recalled the message from Dylan. Her broken heart was now buried, anger replacing the hurt. Something was going on here, though she still didn't know what, but the fact the man she was supposed to spend the rest of her life with had involved Tommy Granger and not her meant that he didn't trust her enough to help him in whatever it was he was doing. Or he had indeed defected and didn't want her involved so had left young Tommy to take the fall. Either way, she had a burning desire to kick the living shit out of her boyfriend and anyone else who might get in her way of finding out the truth. She closed her eyes, drawing several steadying breaths, and the pounding in her ears slowly settled.

"Yeah, that was the second message I sent," said Tommy as he rapidly worked his keyboard.

"The Chief was three minutes later." Sherrie held out her phone and Tommy tapped in the number. He threw his hands up in triumph.

"Got it!"

Sherrie leaned over his shoulder and Fang the other, all three of them staring at the screen. A list of all the phone numbers texted and still to be texted displayed, and a lump formed in Fang's throat as the decrypted list revealed that the last number her beloved had set up a message for, was to her. Her eyes glistened and someone squeezed her forearm. She looked down to see it was Sherrie, smiling at her as she too realized the implications that Fang wasn't willing to forgive just yet, for she had no idea what that message read. Was it the truth of what was really going on? Or was it a farewell? She sighed. "There are a few numbers here I don't recognize. We need to find out who they are."

Tommy nodded then paused. "Now, that's interesting."

"What?" asked both Fang and Sherrie in unison.

"This last message."

Fang's stomach flipped. "What about it?"

"It's set to automatically send on its own."

"Really?" asked Sherrie. "Are any of the others?"

"No, this is the only one."

"Then it must be some sort of failsafe."

Tommy stared up at Sherrie. "What do you mean?"

"Well, if I were him, and this was all part of some mission we haven't been made privy to, I would set up a message to go to Chris if things went wrong, so that he'd know why I did what I did, and that I hadn't betrayed him and my country."

Fang's chest ached with her friend's words. She was right. That's exactly what any of them would have done. But there was another possibility. It was a final apology meant to be sent regardless of what was happening, perhaps explaining why he had betrayed his country and her.

Sherrie gave Fang's arm another squeeze. "Don't go there."

Fang sniffed. "Go where?"

"To that dark place I know you want to go to. Yes, this could mean anything. But for now, I'm going to choose to believe it's a farewell message should the mission go wrong."

Fang turned away, never a fan of showing weakness. No matter what the message represented, whether it was an explanation for why he had done what he had done, becoming a traitor to his own country, or a farewell because his mission had failed and he was now dead, both meant their life together was finished and she would never see him again.

She inhaled deeply and held her breath, her fists clenched, her fingernails digging into the palms of her hands. Sherrie was right. She had to look at this new development in a positive light. There was no way he was a traitor. Something else had to be going on here. And they had to figure out what that was before the hit squad took the only man she had ever loved out of her life permanently.

Operations Center 2, CIA Headquarters

Langley, Virginia

Leroux stared at the screen with the twelve phone numbers decrypted by Tommy Granger, the first six with the dates and times they had been sent by Tommy, and the twelfth message with the date and time it was due to be automatically sent. Precisely 47 hours and 32 minutes from now—less than two days. Whatever Kane was up to, it was all due to be over in some way by that time. The question was, in what way? Would he have secured his deal with the North Koreans and be living in his new country for the rest of his life, or would whatever mission he was truly on have either succeeded or failed, which would likely mean he'd be dead?

Who the last message was being sent to could be the indicator. If Leroux were in the same situation, no matter what the reason, he would want his last communication to be with Sherrie, to tell her one last time how much she meant to him, and how much he loved her.

Tong motioned toward the displays at the front of the operations center. "I've identified most of the numbers. There's you, the Chief, Fang, and his handler. But there's one message that's already been sent that was to a number we have no record of."

Leroux stared at the screen and the six remaining numbers. The last was to Fang, and three of the remaining five were to the Chief. The other two were unidentified, one matching the unidentified number from the six that had already been sent, then one lone number, unidentified and unique in the list. "We need to find out who those numbers belong to."

Child cleared his throat. "Why don't we just call them?"

Tong shook her head. "No, that could tip them off."

"Why? People get wrong numbers all the time."

"Yes, *people* do. But if those unidentified numbers are involved in this, and they all get calls around the same time, if they're coordinating their efforts, they'll know something's going on."

Leroux agreed with Tong's assessment of the situation. If he were Kane, he would have set these numbers up as relays so he could see any activity associated with them, just in case Tommy Granger did exactly what he did—spill the beans. Whatever was going on was a tightly orchestrated plan, and while identifying these numbers was a priority, what was more important was identifying the number that Tommy had been monitoring, each message received triggering the next message sent. Whoever was behind that phone number was the person conducting the entire incident, for Leroux was certain it wasn't his friend making the calls. Someone else was playing maestro, and once they identified who that was, they might take them into custody and find out once and for all just what the hell was going on.

He sucked in a quick breath then issued his orders. "Search every database we've got access to for those numbers. See if we can find any reference. Check telephone company records to see what numbers they've called, what numbers have called them, when they were set up, everything you can, but do *not* ping, call, or in any way interact with those numbers."

"We're on it, boss," replied Tong.

Leroux turned his chair and faced Child. "And I've got a special assignment for you."

Child grinned. "I love special assignments."

"I want you to try to figure out who's been calling the number Tommy Granger has been monitoring. They're the key to this entire thing."

Child cracked his knuckles. "Consider it done."

Leroux rose, and as he passed Tong's station, he said, "Send that list to my phone and send a copy to the Chief. I'm going to brief him and see if he has access to anything we don't."

"So, you think the Chief's holding out on us?"

Leroux chuckled. "Every once in a while, he pulls a rabbit out of his hat. Maybe this will be one of those times." He left the room, heading for the elevators, his mind racing. He had suspected they would discover some piece of the puzzle at Kane's off-the-books operation center, but he never expected to find Tommy Granger, of all people, there. He was the most innocent of the innocent despite his history of hacking when he was a teenager. He was either the perfect patsy, which would mean Kane truly had gone to the dark side, or Kane had needed somebody he could trust that would ask no questions, and who he would somehow make sure was cleared should something go wrong.

He growled as he stabbed the call button for the elevator. They were making progress in the investigation, albeit slowly, but none of the new information shed any light on what Kane's motives were. Was he still one of the good guys, or was he one of the bad?

The doors opened and Therrien barreled into him. "Oh shit, sorry, Chris."

"Don't worry about it." Leroux boarded the elevator and Therrien stepped back on.

"I just got finished talking to three of our docs."

Leroux pressed the button for the Chief's floor. "And? Is there a possible medical explanation?"

Therrien wiggled a hand and shrugged. "Yes and no."

Leroux eyed him. "What's that supposed to mean?"

"It means that, yes, technically, there are a couple of conditions that could explain what's happened, but not only are those conditions incredibly rare, for them to manifest in this way where he seems to have complete control of himself and is fully aware of his past, is pretty much unheard of. I only got one doctor who was willing to say that it was a statistical possibility, and he implied that the only reason he would admit to that officially would be if we wanted a medical excuse to put on the official record for why Kane did what he did. So, bottom line is, I don't think this has anything to do with a medical condition."

Leroux sighed. "I don't know how I feel about that."

"What do you mean?"

"Well, if it's not a medical condition, then he still could be a traitor. But he could also be doing something completely under the radar that, for whatever reason, he didn't want us involved with. But if it was a medical condition, then he'd still be doing whatever it is he's doing, and it would probably be a true defection with no hope in hell of ever getting him back in his right mind."

Therrien's head slowly bobbed. "Yeah, I guess that's one way of looking at it. That hadn't occurred to me. So, what do we do now?"

The elevator chimed and the doors opened. "I'm going to see the Chief. You report back to ops. Sonya will bring you up to speed. There've been some developments."

"Well, that's good, at least."

Leroux rolled his eyes. "You would think, wouldn't you?" He headed down the corridor then through the guarded doors that led to senior management. He smiled at Morrison's executive assistant. "Is he in?"

She smiled back. "He always is for you, Chris." She picked up the phone and pressed a button. "Chris Leroux to see you, sir...yes, sir." She hung up the phone and gestured toward the door to the inner sanctum. "Go on in."

"Thanks." He entered and found Morrison behind his desk, staring at his laptop. The Chief pointed at an empty chair and Leroux sat.

"I'm just looking at these numbers you sent me. What do you make of the fact the last message is meant for Lee Fang?"

"Hard to say, sir. I know that if I didn't think I'd ever see Sherrie again, I'd want to send her a message, explaining what I had done and why we're saying goodbye."

"So, it still gives us no indication as to what he's up to."

"I don't think so, except that whatever is happening he expects to be over with in less than two days."

Morrison peered at the screen again. "Huh, I missed that. So, he either thinks that he'll be past a point of no return, or dead by the time that message is sent."

Leroux offered up a more positive spin. "Or he thinks it'll all be over and he'll be safely back home in time to stop that message from being sent."

"A rather optimistic way of looking at it, don't you think?"

"He's my best friend, sir." Leroux's voice cracked. "I…" He dipped his head and pressed a knuckle against the bridge of his nose, hard. "I'm sorry, sir."

"It's okay, son."

Leroux sniffed hard and blinked his eyes clear. "I have to try to think positively. I have to believe he's innocent in all this and is either doing this against his will or doing this for a reason that he thinks puts him on the side of right."

Morrison sighed then leaned back in his chair, steepling his fingers. "I've known Dylan a long time. Not as well as you, obviously, though operationally, I've known him longer. He's always been a pain in my ass, but he's never given me reason to believe he'd betray his country."

Leroux cleared his throat. "Well, there was that one time."

Morrison peered at him. "When?"

"With the North Koreans. Remember when those scientists and their families were kidnapped?"

Morrison's jaw dropped for a moment before he snapped it shut. "I can't believe I'd forgotten about that. I actually put a kill order out on him."

"Yes, sir. You don't think…" Leroux's voice drifted off as his mind raced again with new possibilities.

"What is it? What's that famous gut of yours telling you?"

"I'm not sure. But it is a little coincidental, isn't it? That once again, it involves North Korea and kidnapped scientists?"

"You mean he's helping them recruit for their International Cooperation Center?"

Leroux shrugged. "Could be. Think about it. What does he have to offer to the North Koreans? Information is kept pretty compartmentalized in this business, so he might be able to name a few undercover operatives in their midst, explain the inner workings of the CIA and various other agencies, but that's all. Information that's time-sensitive, codes, passwords, everything was changed the moment we identified him as the person crossing that bridge. We pulled out operatives and other assets. I don't think that type of knowledge is very useful in this situation. But in less than twenty-four hours of him defecting, we've already got one of our top scientists kidnapped and on his way to North Korea. Access to people like that is worth a hell of a lot more than the names of a few assets, and their knowledge is timeless. He could dole out a name every few months to ensure they keep their end of the bargain."

"But how did he get access to those names?" Morrison rose and paced behind his desk. "Scientists like that are kept on very short leashes and are almost never mentioned by name in any reports. Only director level and above in the Agency can even find out who these people are. Kane doesn't have the clearance."

"Well, somebody obviously does, or he's bluffing them and just got lucky with the one name."

Morrison paused, turning toward him. "So, he somehow came across this one name and uses it to get him on the good side of his new masters?" He shook his head before returning to his chair. "That doesn't make sense. If he's only got one name, or let's say even two or three, he'll quickly run out and the North Koreans will lose interest. They might even execute him."

"That depends on what he promised. He might have only promised them the one person. And if this guy is as good as his file suggests, that one person could be enough to get their nuclear energy program up and running, which is a game-changer for them. That one name could be enough to secure his future with them."

Morrison frowned. "Perhaps, though would you trust the North Koreans to keep their word if you only had one thing to offer them?"

"No, I wouldn't. But then again, I wouldn't be defecting either. If he actually has defected, then he might not be thinking straight, or he's been forced into some rash action that he hasn't thought through."

Morrison squeezed the bridge of his nose, closing his eyes. "Or he's there for a very specific reason that we don't know, and this specific scientist was chosen for a reason we don't know." The phone on his desk beeped and he grabbed the receiver. "Yes? Okay, put her through."

Leroux rose to leave but Morrison waved him off, though pressed a finger to his lips to indicate he should remain silent.

"Hi Carol, how are you doing?...I've had better days...Wait a minute, what?"

Leroux tensed at the change in tone.

"And is that decision final?...Well, I'm sorry, ma'am, but I think that's the wrong decision, the absolute wrong decision. I understand that the president disagrees, but if you shoot that plane down in international airspace, half the world's going to go apeshit, and it'll be open season on any of our own rendition flights. Right now, in the intelligence world, it's basically agreed that if you get them on your plane and into international airspace, they're yours. If you want Burkett dead, then let us take him out on the ground in North Korea, then it never makes the evening news or the morning papers. I'd be happy to talk to the president if you think it would help...very well, ma'am, I'll be there momentarily." Morrison hung up the phone then grabbed at his temples. "This is getting out of hand."

Leroux wasn't sure what to say. He had just been privy to one side of a conversation he was never supposed to hear.

Morrison stared at him. "The president has ordered the plane Burkett is on shot down."

Leroux's chest tightened and his stomach flipped. "Sir, if that plane is shot down, no matter what the reason Dylan's over there, good or bad, it'll mean his death. If we show that we're willing to kill anybody that he names, he becomes worthless to them, and if he's up to something, he needs Burkett there for some reason. You need to convince them to let Burkett arrive in North Korea so we can let this play out and see what's going on."

Morrison rose. "That's just what I'm going to try to do. I'm meeting the director now, then going straight into a conference call with the president." He paused at the door. "Any word on that medical theory?"

Leroux shook his head. "Nothing I'd hang a career on, sir. It's an extremely remote possibility, but we do have a doctor willing to say it is possible if we need plausible deniability over what triggered Kane to do what he's done."

Morrison held the doorknob for a moment as he considered what had just been said. "Interesting idea. Keep that one under your hat. We just might have to use it if this stays the shitshow that it is."

Over the Pacific Ocean

International Airspace

Major Choe grabbed on to the nearest headrest as their plane jerked hard to the left. A roaring sound ripped past them, and as the plane leveled out, he and the others rushed to the windows. And he cursed. Two F-22 Raptors had just buzzed them and were now banking sharply. They would soon be coming up behind them for the kill.

"Major, report to the cockpit."

Choe headed for the cockpit then rapped twice. The door was opened from the inside. "What's going on?"

The pilot was busy on his headset, leaving the copilot to fill him in. "We just got buzzed by two fighter jets. American F-22s, I think. Now they're demanding we follow them back to Joint Base Elmendorf-Richardson."

"We're not going to, I assume."

The pilot shook his head. "Not unless you order me to. If we turn around, Command will make sure we're dead, and we'll never know when it's coming. At least this way, we die here and now in a blaze of glory, heroes of the motherland."

Choe slapped the pilot on the back. "Good man. If by some miracle we make it out of this, I'm putting you up for a commendation."

The pilot laughed. "You might want to radio that one in so they can award it to me posthumously. These guys sound angry, and I get the distinct feeling they're not going to take no for an answer."

Tracer fire sprayed past the cockpit, meaning countless more rounds they couldn't see were tearing apart the air just ahead of them. This was unprecedented. They were in international airspace in a civilian registered aircraft and were being fired upon. Yes, everyone on this airplane was North Korean military with the exception of their captive, but how the Americans could be certain of that, he had no idea. They could only have their suspicions. For all the Americans knew, this was an actual charter flight and the crew were innocent, completely unaware of what was going on.

It gave him an idea.

"Your cover is Chinese, isn't it?"

The pilot nodded.

"Then tell them that. Tell them you are Chinese and you don't trust any American military. You're going to land in China as planned and they can take it up with the Chinese government. Stick to that story, because you're right, the moment we turn around, Command will be planning our funerals in Pyongyang."

"It's worth a try. Let's hope the Supreme Leader and the Great Leader are watching down upon us."

114

"Let's hope." Choe leaned in. "But just in case, fly this thing like you normally would. No evasive maneuvers, don't change altitude, don't increase or decrease your speed. Just stick to the flight plan." Choe stepped out of the cockpit and closed the door. He pulled out his satellite phone and held it out for their prisoner. "Call whoever you have to call and tell them to back off."

Burkett stared up at him from his seat and snickered. "Nothing I can say will change their minds."

"Why is that?"

"Because they probably read my file."

"And what does your file say?"

"I'm sure it says a lot of things, but two things are of importance. The first is that I'm all about the work."

Choe's eyes narrowed. "What does that mean?"

"It means I don't care who I'm working for, as long as I'm allowed to work. I live for the science, so whether I'm doing that science for the country I was born in, or for the country that imprisons me, I really don't care. In a hundred years, in a thousand years, it won't matter. All that matters is that the science moves forward. Your country chose wisely when it chose me. Most other scientists would hold out, try to trick you, refuse to cooperate. Me?" Burkett shrugged. "I simply don't care about such things. Geopolitics never interested me. All I care about is the science.

"How many German scientists after World War II, even *during* World War II, worked with the allies on the nuclear bomb, then worked with the Americans and the Russians on their rocket programs?

They didn't care either. They were there for the science, though I will agree self-preservation played some part in most of their cases, and self-preservation plays a part for me as well. I must survive. I must continue to work. Whether it benefits your country now and mine in a decade or in a century, I don't care as long as somebody benefits and the science pushes forward.

"Minds like mine are rare, and they come once or twice in a generation. It can't be wasted. It will cost humanity far too much. In time, all countries fall, all hatreds end, all alliances crumble. It's the nature of things. Eventually, any knowledge that I develop for you will make it into the hands of others and spread throughout the world, and the human species will advance because of it. You kidnapping me can't be allowed to interfere with that work."

"And what's the second thing?"

"Your file will indicate that I'm an arrogant asshole that nobody likes. I can guarantee you, there will be nobody back home agitating on my behalf. Once you have me, you have me, and they know that."

"If you're so important to the future of mankind, what makes you think they wouldn't try to get you back?"

"Because those making the decisions are morons."

"Excuse me?"

"They're government. Politicians and bureaucrats. You can't expect them to make decisions based on what's best for mankind. They make decisions based on what's best for them and their immediate political future. I fully expect that we'll be dead in the next few minutes unless someone far more intelligent than would normally be involved is able to change their minds and think past the immediate problem. Washington needs a grandmaster chess player in the game instead of all the checkers players they normally have."

Choe pocketed the satphone. This man wasn't going to make any calls, and even if he did, his unparalleled arrogance would likely get them shot down sooner than they otherwise would.

The pilot's voice crackled over the speakers. "It looks like they're lining up for their shot. Say your goodbyes now. This should be over quickly. It's been an honor, gentlemen."

Burkett closed his eyes and leaned his head back, his slight smile suggesting he was pleased he had been proven correct. Choe sat in his seat and pulled out his wallet. He retrieved a photo and ran three fingers across its surface, touching the faces of his wife and two daughters that he hadn't seen in years. His assignment as a sleeper agent in the United States meant a tremendous sacrifice for his family. The Americans preferred to send agents that had no family ties, but with North Korea it was the exact opposite. Family ties guaranteed you'd return. The temptations of life in the West were great, but unlike the average American, he had been trained to pay attention to the inequalities. To see how the poor were left to rot in their own filth, how the elderly were abandoned by their families and the system they had paid for all their lives. In North Korea, everyone was treated equally. Everyone was provided for equally. Yes, life could be hard, but no one was left behind.

He missed his family dearly and he couldn't wait to see them, yet now he'd have to wait to see them in the afterlife, if there even was such a thing. This was supposed to be his last mission. He had been activated, his identity compromised. He was supposed to come home a hero with the rewards promised him for his selfless service to the state, and be reunited with his wife and daughters.

"Brace yourselves."

He closed his eyes and thought of the promise he had made to his wife the day he left. A promise he was about to break.

I'll be back. Trust me.

Operations Center 2, CIA Headquarters

Langley, Virginia

Leroux burst into the operations center and pointed at Tong. "Bring up Secure Pentagon Feed Bravo Victor Five-Four-Five."

Tong tapped at her keyboard as Leroux came to a stop in the center of the room, turning to face the displays. "It's audio only."

"Let me hear it and show me everything we've got on that plane."

The speakers crackled overhead. "Stand by, Hotel-Sierra-One. We're still waiting for confirmation, over."

"Copy that, standing by."

"What's going on?" asked Tong as the main displays filled with various feeds showing the current location of the charter plane carrying Burkett. "The president has just ordered them to splash that plane."

Child cursed. "Then you might as well tell Bravo Team to turn around. The North Koreans are going to kill Kane the moment they get word we're willing to kill anyone he targets."

"The Chief and I are of the same opinion. He's meeting with the director right now then heading into a teleconference with the president to try to get him to change his mind."

"But should we?" asked Therrien. "I mean, not to sound cold-hearted here, but if we don't take out that plane, the North Koreans are going to have access to one of the top nuclear physicists in the world. Isn't the risk of that too dangerous to let happen just because we're not sure what Kane's up to? I mean, let's be honest here. If this were almost any other person, we wouldn't even be thinking twice."

Leroux bristled at the accusation then calmed himself, for Therrien was right. They were biased, especially himself, which was why his team wouldn't be involved in the final kill order. Morrison didn't trust him to give the order, and frankly, he didn't trust himself. Kane was his best friend, the only friend he had ever had, and killing him was unthinkable. "You're right. If it were any other asset that we weren't as familiar with, we wouldn't be having these conversations, but there's a reason for that and it's not entirely bias. We know Kane. Hell, I've known him for years. Since high school. And he's my best friend. I can't say that about any other asset. In fact, most of the assets we deal with, I've never met and never spoken to outside of the communications you hear in this room. That means I don't know them. You don't know them. So, we have to go entirely based upon the facts at hand. But in this case, we do know him. We know it's completely out of character. We know there were no warning signs. So, it opens up the possibility that something else is going on here. Should we ignore what we know about the man just because normally we wouldn't have that type of human intel?"

Therrien raised his hands slightly as he sighed. "You're right. We shouldn't ignore it. All I'm saying is that maybe we need to compartmentalize things a bit. Look at *this* situation and ignore Kane. Let's assess the risk to our country and to the world. Should this scientist be allowed to reach North Korea?"

Child grunted. "Dude, I hope you're never in charge if somebody kidnaps me."

"What's that supposed to mean?"

"It means we're not talking about a hard drive filled with data here, we're talking about an innocent human being. And we should just kill him?"

"We're prepared to kill Kane and we know him."

"Yes, but Kane might not be innocent. This guy is. He's done nothing wrong, and we're about to blow him out of the sky? Doesn't he at least deserve a chance?"

"I don't think any of that matters anymore," said Tong, pointing at the speakers overhead.

Leroux cocked an ear to hear what he had missed.

"—repeat. Abort! Abort! Abort! Return to base. Acknowledge, over!"

"Copy that, Command. Abort order acknowledged. Flight Hotel-Sierra returning to base, over."

Leroux's shoulders slumped as he exhaled heavily. Burkett would live, at least for now, and while the president had been willing to kill the man, the North Koreans would assume they had called America's bluff and won. It should hopefully mean they would trust that anyone Kane named in the future could also be successfully brought in without worrying that the American government would shoot down an entire airplane.

He had a feeling, though, the North Koreans would be more careful next time. This was the test. A snatch and grab of an extremely valuable asset, and America had let them do it. Unfortunately, by reacting the way they had, they had rendered useless the test he had planned. If the plane had landed in China, then it meant the North Koreans were trying to hide the fact they had kidnapped Burkett, which suggested Kane telling Morrison meant he was working independently of the North Koreans. But now that the North Koreans were fully aware that the American government was aware, there was no longer any need for them to land in China. They would simply land in North Korea now, and there would be no way to tell if it was the plan all along.

He sat at his station and closed his eyes for a moment. He yawned then checked his watch. "Okay. We're due to switch shifts soon. Prepare your briefing reports for your replacements on anything you want them to continue working on. Remember, we've been sequestered, so rack time, mealtime, happy times are all within the building. No one's allowed to leave and all outgoing calls will be monitored. Everyone report back here in eight hours, bright-eyed and bushy-tailed, so we're ready to deal with that plane landing and Bravo Team getting into position. Get your rest because I don't know when we'll be sleeping again." His phone vibrated with a secure message from Sherrie.

We've got something. Need to talk to you on secure line.

For her to want him to communicate in a way the CIA couldn't monitor had to mean she had discovered something about the suspected mole, and the very idea there was somebody within their midst that they couldn't trust, shook him to his core.

Kane's off-the-books Operations Center

Outside Bethesda, Maryland

Sherrie stared at the screen, scrolling up and down through the phone records that Tommy had managed to gather. The guy was an extraordinary hacker and could gain access to pretty much any system in the world if given enough time. Telephone company records were child's play. The messages signaling him to send the corresponding outgoing message were all coming in over a satellite feed using one of the dishes on the roof of the container they were in. That had made it slightly more challenging according to Tommy, but because Kane didn't own his own satellite, every data packet was wrapped, giving the source.

That source, of course, wasn't the originating phone. It was merely the originating terminal that had sent the data packet to the satellite. It had taken him some time, but he had finally found the originating phone, and the implications were as horrifying as they had feared.

A secure phone buzzed at the workstation and she grabbed the receiver. "Hello?"

"Hey, it's me. I'm secure at this end."

She checked the indicators on the panel, nothing showing any evidence of a suspected tap. "We're good here."

"What's so important you have me breaking protocol?"

Sherrie smiled at her boyfriend's question as she stared at the screen again. "We tracked the source phone number."

"I'm not going to like this, am I?"

She shook her head. "No. Tommy managed to find out that it was a burner phone activated three weeks ago."

"Do we know by whom?"

"No, looks like it was paid for and activated with cash."

"Anything from the usage that could help us?"

"This is what you're not going to like. Every single one of the messages sent here were all sent by this phone. It looks like they would turn on the phone, send the message, then turn it off. We're talking a minute at a time, tops."

"And the location?"

"Every one of the messages was transmitted from a cellphone tower at Langley."

Leroux cursed. "I knew there was a mole, but I was hoping it was in DC. So, this means Dylan's working with someone inside headquarters."

"Do you think they could be North Korean?"

"Anything's possible. It all depends on what side of things he's on. If he is indeed working for the North Koreans, then using one of their assets is a possibility, though it wouldn't really make much sense."

Sherrie's eyes narrowed. "What do you mean?"

"I mean, none of these messages benefit the North Koreans, so why would they agree to have one of their assets assist in sending them? Also, if it were a North Korean asset, it would mean he had made contact with them before he arrived on that bridge. If that were the case, that's not how he would have made entry. He would've just flown to China using one of his covers, then met them at the border. He wouldn't have had to parachute in. Everything he's done so far was dramatic. He wanted to be seen. He wanted us to know what he was doing, and there's no way the North Koreans would've agreed to that."

"So, what are we saying?"

There was a pause as her boyfriend collected his thoughts. "What I'm saying is that I don't believe he's using a North Korean asset. He's using somebody inside the Agency."

"Wittingly?"

"It would have to be wittingly. He's not telling them when to send the messages. The mole is monitoring events then sending the message to Tommy."

"So then we might have two traitors."

"Possibly. Though if Kane is still on our side, that person could be helping him because it's the right thing to do. We need to figure out who the hell that person is because they might be able to tell us what's actually going on."

"But how do we find out if they've always got their phone turned off?"

"We're going to have to be ready for when the next message is sent."

"But how are we going to know when that is?"

"My guess is the moment that plane crosses into North Korean airspace, we're going to receive a message."

"What are you going to do in the meantime?"

"Get some sleep. Call me if anything happens and have Tommy keep searching to see if there was any other activity with that phone. Also, have him check and see if any other phones were purchased and activated around the same time in the same area. We might get lucky."

"I'll tell him."

"I'm going to get some sleep and I'll talk to you later."

"Okay. Love you."

"Love you too."

Sherrie ended the call then turned to the others. "We've got work to do."

Pothong Riverside Terraced Residential District

Pyongyang, North Korea

"Mr. Kane, I'd like you to meet Yang Kwan."

Kane smiled broadly at the gorgeous woman standing in front of him. Pak had come through in a big way, and if she were half as intelligent as she was beautiful, she would definitely help pass the time.

Kwan bowed deeply. "It's a pleasure to meet you, Mr. Kane."

Kane returned the bow though not as deep. He was, after all, the master here. "It's a pleasure to meet you. Please, call me Dylan." He reached out and took her by the hand, clasping it in both of his. "I hope over time we'll become good friends."

She smiled. "That is my wish as well."

She was too confident to be in the sex trade—she was an intelligence asset, there was no doubt about it. She probably knew a thousand ways to kill him that he'd have no defense against. She would keep him on his toes—she'd be trained to keep him happy, sexually and emotionally, but also to test him.

He'd have to be careful.

But she was perfect for his purposes.

He let go of her hand then surveyed his new digs. They were basic, but clean. It appeared to be a one-bedroom apartment, and the complex he had driven up to seemed modern and well maintained. It would seem his captors were making an attempt to keep him happy by American standards. Yet this was very basic, and though perhaps recently built, the stylings were Soviet-era—forty or fifty years out of date with a few modern touches like a flat panel screen mounted on one wall across from the couch.

"This is decent. I assume, however, once our final agreement is made, I'll be upgraded to something better."

Pak stepped deeper into the apartment. "I assure you, this is one of the finest buildings available."

Kane turned to the major and gave him a look. "You and I both know there's better. And with what I'll be doing for your country, it's a small price to pay."

"I'll bring it up to my superiors that you're not satisfied."

Kane waved him off. "No, no, no, no. That's not what I said. I said, this is fine for now, so for the moment I'm satisfied. This beats the hell out of the prison cell I spent last night in." He took Kwan's hand again and turned to her. "You wouldn't believe what they had me in. It was absolutely horrendous."

She smiled. "I can imagine so. But you're here now, and you've got me to take care of you."

Kane kissed her hand. "You are far better looking than the prison guard I had last night."

She giggled. "I should hope so."

He turned to Pak. "When does the flight land?"

"In six hours."

"And what will you be doing with him?"

"There'll be a short debriefing where his new situation will be explained to him and the consequences of not cooperating. Then he'll be introduced to his new coworkers."

Kane glanced at Kwan. "Is it safe to speak in front of her?"

"You can speak freely."

The confirmation affirmed what he suspected—Kwan was an intelligence asset. "Good. I prefer to know where I stand." He continued to hold her hand. "One of the reasons I chose Dr. Burkett for this, shall we say, assignment, is his rather unique beliefs. He believes that the science must be advanced at all costs, so he doesn't care who he's working for. He believes that he's ultimately working for mankind. He is so self-absorbed that he couldn't care less that he's now working for North Korea as opposed to the United States. I think you'll find him very compliant."

Pak agreed. "That does match with the initial reports I've received from the extraction team."

"One more thing, though. He's arrogant. Unbelievably arrogant, which makes him come off as an asshole. He likes to work alone. So, you might find him a bit incommunicative, especially with anybody he considers less intelligent than him. Understood?"

Pak smiled slightly. "But from what you've told me, we're all less intelligent than him."

Kane laughed. "Major, we're all morons compared to him. But remember, even your top scientists are probably far less intelligent than him, and he's going to let them know it. Just be prepared for him to be less than cooperative if you attempt to challenge his knowledge. Just let him do his work. I'd be willing to bet he'll have your reactor up and running in well under a year, and Pyongyang will have seen its last blackout."

Kwan bounced on her toes. "That would be wonderful!"

Pak agreed, though not quite so boisterously. "Indeed. Then I'll leave you two to get to know each other. I'll be back in the morning to pick you up."

"Sounds good." Kane extended a hand and Pak shook it. "Goodnight, Major."

"Goodnight, Mr. Kane."

Pak left the apartment and Kwan locked the door behind him. She turned, her back pressed against the door as she stared at him seductively. "You have no idea how much I've been looking forward to this assignment since I saw your photo."

Kane approached her then pressed his body against hers. "Then I guess I shouldn't make you wait."

She reached up and grabbed his head, pulling him closer as her eyes closed. He kissed her gently at first then more fervently, and as his arousal grew, his heart ached with the enormous guilt he felt for betraying the only woman he had ever loved.

Temporary Staff Quarters, CIA Headquarters

Langley, Virginia

"Time to wake up, sleepyhead."

Leroux flinched then stretched as he remembered where he was—one of the private sleeping quarters inside the CIA Headquarters complex. It was dark in the windowless room, though the door to the hallway was slightly ajar, the light silhouetting Sherrie standing by his bedside. He reached up and grabbed her hand, pulling her closer, and she gasped as their lips met. He was quickly aroused and grabbed her other hand, bringing it toward Chris Jr. when she abruptly yanked away.

"Chris, it's me!"

His heart nearly stopped at Tong's voice. "Oh my God!" He reached over and flicked on the light, revealing a slightly disheveled Tong, her chest heaving, her eyes wide, her mouth agape. He smacked his forehead. "Oh my God, I'm so sorry, Sonya. I thought you were Sherrie."

"I kind of wish I was," she muttered.

"What was that?"

She blushed. "Nothing. Sorry, I should have said something sooner."

He laughed. "Sherrie is going to find this hilarious."

Tong's eyes shot wide. "You're not going to tell her, are you?"

He paused. "Yeah, you're right. Dylan would find it hilarious, Sherrie might decide she has to kill you."

Tong's jaw dropped and he gave her a look.

"That was a joke."

The jaw snapped shut. "Not a good one."

He shrugged. "I'm usually the butt of the joke, not the one cracking it."

Her expression softened. "I think you're funny."

He grinned. "You have to say that. I'm your boss."

She clasped her hands in front of her, staring down at them. "I like to think we're friends."

He began to stand when something down below reminded him of what had just happened moments before. He immediately sat back down, grabbing his pillow and covering the evidence.

She giggled. "Must have been one hell of a kiss."

It was his turn to flush. "I guess so. Maybe we're not going to mention this to anyone."

"I think that's probably best. I'll see you in ops?"

"Yes."

She stepped toward the door when he stopped her.

"Oh, and Sonya?"

"Yeah?"

"You better fix your lipstick."

She stepped over to the mirror and snorted. "Yep, if anybody saw me coming out of here like this, we'd both be in front of HR." She fixed her lipstick then pointed at his own lips. "You better wash that face, mister, or you'll have some splainin' to do."

He wiped his lips with the back of his hand and laughed. "Thanks. Now, you better get out of here before HR *does* show up with their clipboard."

Tong grinned at him then left, closing the door behind her. Leroux locked it and struggled with his pants, battling the wagger, surprised at how turned on he still was and how his mind kept picturing what could have happened if they hadn't stopped. He loved Sherrie, was completely loyal to her, and would never cheat on her, but what had just happened was probably the most exciting thing that had ever happened outside of his love life with Sherrie.

He checked himself in the mirror, wiping the last bit of lipstick from the corner of his mouth, then checked to make sure he could walk normally.

And sighed.

There's no way you're telling Sherrie about this.

He closed his eyes.

I just hope that one day I get to tell Dylan.

He checked his watch. The flight was due to enter Chinese airspace in an hour. If they changed their route, which he was certain they would, it meant a message was probably going to be sent soon thereafter, so he would have to be ready. He opened the door and stepped into the corridor, several of his team emerging from their own rooms.

"Hey, boss," said Child as he walked up to him. "Get any sleep?"

"A few hours. You?"

"Slept like a baby. I don't know what it is about the beds here, but I always sleep better here than at my apartment."

"Talk to building maintenance. Maybe they can tell you who their mattress supplier is and you can get the make."

Child eyeballed him for a moment. "That's not a bad idea, but I can't afford government prices. You just know we pay five times what they're worth."

"I didn't say buy it from us, I said find out who we're buying from so they can tell you what type it is. You might get lucky."

"I'm doing that the minute this op is over." Child stepped on the elevator but Leroux hung back. "You're not coming?"

"I have a meeting. I'll join you guys in about fifteen minutes."

"Quick meeting."

"Yep." The doors closed and Leroux took the next elevator, pressing the button that would take him to the quartermaster.

There was equipment he needed to sign out.

CIA Headquarters
Langley, Virginia

Sonya Tong stepped into the bathroom stall and locked the door. She was giddy, her entire body shaking from the adrenaline pumping through her veins. When Leroux had pulled her in, she wasn't certain what was going on, but when their lips met, her heart had gone into overdrive and she nearly passed out from the shock and excitement. She would have let it continue, but when he took her other hand, it was about to escalate into something that went beyond innocent mistake. It could have destroyed the friendship they had, but God, she would have loved to have kept going, to go all the way.

But that wasn't in the cards, and she wasn't that kind of girl.

She still had feelings for him, and at the moment, she was utterly infatuated with him yet again, but that would fade with the memory. Well, that was the theory. She had a feeling there was no way this memory would fade any time soon, and she'd be using it to fire up her imagination the first chance she got to be alone.

She was alone.

She groaned as her hand slid down her body, then almost yelped as a door opened. She inhaled sharply, straightening her clothes before flushing the toilet. She counted to ten then unlocked the stall. Avril Casey, one of the analyst supervisors who managed an op center crew like Leroux, smiled at her in the mirror.

"You look a little out of sorts."

Tong's cheeks burned and she forced herself toward the sink. "It's just the op we're on."

"Oh yeah? What have they got you working on?"

Tong shook her head. "Sorry. Classified."

Casey grunted. "Aren't they all? Did you spend the night?"

"Yeah, we all did. We're sequestered."

Casey's eyebrows rose slightly. "Wow. Must be one hell of an op."

"You have no idea."

Casey dried her hands. "Well, good luck with it. I hope it turns out well."

"You and me both."

Casey left the bathroom and Tong washed her face and hands then took a moment to straighten her hair and reapply her lipstick. She wondered just how she would face Leroux without the entire room knowing they had been lip-locked only minutes ago, and she almost had his little guy in her hand.

She giggled.

Thank God I stopped him.

She headed for the door, the she-devil on the other shoulder scolding her for not having taken advantage of the opportunity. She growled at herself.

I have to get a boyfriend.

"Or at least get laid," whispered the devil in her ear.

Pothong Riverside Terraced Residential District

Pyongyang, North Korea

There was no denying the sex was good. In fact, the sex was incredible. But sex was just sex without love. Kane would trade a thousand nights with Kwan for just one more night with Fang. He had always known this would be the hardest part, hurting the ones he loved, especially her, but he had no choice.

Today was the big day.

The extraction team would be arriving shortly with their prize, then his entire future depended upon what came next. He was counting on the supreme arrogance of the man to carry the day and win him the confidence of his new masters, but something else would be happening today as well. He had no doubt a hit squad had been sent to take him out and that they would be in position to do so today. He would have to be on the lookout and take all the necessary precautions. The best would be sent and the best was Bravo Team. The question was, what were their orders? There was only one possible set that likely would have been approved by the president himself.

Kill him at the earliest opportunity.

Kwan stirred beside him and smiled. "I can't remember the last time I had so much fun," she cooed.

"Neither can I," he lied. "I think you and I are going to get along just fine."

"How much time do we have?" she asked.

He checked his watch. "We have to be ready to leave in an hour."

She grinned at him mischievously. "I think that's plenty of time for a little stress reliever, and then I'll make you breakfast while you shower."

"I don't think…"

She disappeared under the sheets and changed his mind, his eyes rolling into the back of his head as he groaned. Today might very well be his last day on earth, so he might as well enjoy it. Yet as she worked her magic, he closed his eyes and imagined he was back home in his apartment with the woman he loved, and not here in this hellhole of a dictatorship with a woman who meant nothing to him and would never mean anything to him, and always would be someone he was merely playing a part with.

And for the first time since he'd been here, he broke, and a single tear rolled free, down the side of his face and past his ear.

Operations Center 2, CIA Headquarters

Langley, Virginia

Leroux entered the operations center, racked with guilt. He smiled weakly at Tong, who made brief eye contact, her cheeks flushed.

Yup, it's going to be awkward.

But kissing her wasn't the cause of his guilt, it was what was in his bag. They had a mole in the Agency working for Kane, and they had to find out who it was. Thousands upon thousands of people worked in this building, but very few of them were privy to what was going on. Outside of his team, there were only a handful. The mole could be anyone, but that mole would need access to the same intel his team had to know when certain key events occurred, and when the messages should be triggered. It should mean that the mole was either a member of his team, which he prayed it wasn't, or one of the handful of upper management aware of what was going on. Yet those assumptions were based upon the handful not sharing the information they were privy to with others.

He placed his bag on his workstation and took a seat, his mind growing more desperate as he realized that the handful had the potential to be much bigger. If he just thought of the Chief, what information was his aide privy to? Did he share information with other senior analysts or analyst supervisors? Leroux was privy to information that he shouldn't be because the Chief trusted him and valued his opinion, but he was certain that domain wasn't exclusively his. There could be any number of people aware of what was going on, but for now, his immediate concern was whether he could trust everyone in the room he now sat in.

"How far is that plane from North Korean airspace?"

"It depends," replied Tong. "If they make the course change, they can be there in as little as five minutes. I suspect they'll wait until the last moment before they do it, though."

"If they do it at all," muttered Child.

Leroux ignored it. His heart was racing, his palms sweaty. Within minutes, he could know whether one of his own team was the mole. He couldn't believe it was possible, but then again, he never would have believed his best friend could be a traitor, or that someone like Tommy Granger could have been recruited to help. If it was a member of his team, they had to be willing participants. Tommy had the excuse of not knowing what he was doing—whoever was sending the messages to trigger his efforts knew full well what was going on.

There was no way this person could plead ignorance.

143

He had signed out a signal scanner from the quartermaster and it was now running, scanning for any signal in the room. If the triggering message was sent and it was from within these four walls, he would know, then security would be called in and everyone searched. And while he would love to know who was sending the messages, he prayed that the seventh message due to be sent wasn't picked up by the scanner.

"They're changing course," announced Tong.

Leroux looked up to see the red line tracing the route now showing a sharp turn directly for North Korean airspace.

"ETA two minutes."

Child spun. "Does this tell us anything?"

Leroux shook his head. "No, not anymore. As soon as we intercepted them, they knew we knew. There's no point in trying to hide it now. They just want to get him safely on the ground as quickly as possible. Any projection as to where they're going to land?"

"There are several possibilities along that route," replied Tong. "But if I had to hazard a guess, I would say Sunchon. It's military, just outside of Pyongyang, and close to their nuclear reactor. It minimizes his exposure to any hit team we might send in." She pointed at the screen. "They're in North Korean airspace."

Leroux watched as the flashing indicator passed across the dotted line, indicating the territorial airspace of North Korea. Shooting them down now would be an act of war. Kane's first arranged kidnapping was now a success, but what that meant was anybody's guess. If the North Koreans managed to hang on to Burkett, it could change the country's prospects dramatically and quickly. Stable nuclear power could improve the lives of millions living within the world's most repressive regime, and just that one accomplishment could be enough to solidify Kane's standing in his new homeland. This one success could mean his friend would disappear permanently within hours, either dead because he was of no more use, or enjoying whatever benefits he had negotiated.

He growled. It just made no sense. What could the North Koreans possibly offer him that he couldn't get here?

"You okay, boss?" asked Child from behind him.

Leroux batted a hand. "Just frustrated with the situation." His phone beeped, indicating a secure message. He brought up the messenger and read the update from Sherrie.

Relay message received. It's for the Chief. How do we proceed?

He quickly replied, his heart hammering.

Send messages as per normal routine.

A thumbs-up was returned. He pulled the USB key from the scanner and plugged it into his workstation. A list of everything it had recorded appeared with the software's best guess as to what each device was. Everyone had a cellphone, some even had tablets, Fitbits, and various other devices that emitted signals, but all he cared about was one specific cellphone and whether it had been activated in the past minute or so. He typed in the number and the software scanned the recorded data then indicated a negative search result.

His shoulders relaxed with relief, though he had to be sure. He sent a message to Sherrie.

Has Tommy confirmed that it was sent from the same cellphone?

Affirmative.

Give me the exact time the packet was sent.

There was a pause before a date and time to the millisecond was received. He sorted all the signals, looking to see if anything had been sent at the same time, for there was still a possibility there was another relay happening, but he found nothing. From the moment the plane had crossed into North Korean airspace and when the message had been sent, nothing had been transmitted from the room.

He sent another message.

Confirm the cellphone tower location.

Same as the others. Langley-based.

He exhaled loudly and his chest ached. His people were cleared. They weren't involved and the guilt that now racked him over being forced to test their loyalty was overwhelming. Now the question was whether he told them what he had just done. Everyone was fully aware of the messages and that there were few in the loop that would know when to send them. They had to be suspecting each other, and he had noticed that as this operation progressed, the usual chatter among the team had waned and was almost nonexistent now.

The trust that was always there was being tested.

He rose and turned to the group. "May I have everyone's attention, please?"

Everyone stopped, all eyes now on him, something that at one time would have rendered him speechless. He pulled the scanner from his bag and held it up.

"This is a signal scanner. It's been monitoring all communications within this room since I entered a few minutes ago." He held up a hand. "Don't worry, I haven't been reading any of your sexts or anything like that, I've been scanning for the cellphone that's been sending the trigger signals. You'll be happy to know, just as I suspected, it was not coming from anyone in this room. A message *was* sent just after the plane crossed into North Korean airspace, and it was sent from this building, but not this room. So, if any of you have been doubting your colleagues, rest easy. None of you are in cahoots with Kane."

Child raised a hand as if he were still in high school. "Well, there's still one of us that could be."

Leroux regarded the young man, puzzled. "Who?"

"You. You could be lying to us."

Leroux laughed then pulled the USB key from his station and tossed it to Child. "Check it yourself." He pointed at one of the other analysts. "You watch him. *I* won't read any of your messages, but I wouldn't trust him."

Uncomfortable laughter rippled through the room.

Child stared at his screen then a hand shot up. "I've got dick pics!"

Half the room rushed toward his workstation, the other half roared with laughter and Leroux smiled as he headed for the door, his team's unity restored. He opened the door and took one last look back, making eye contact with Tong, who smiled broadly at him. He returned it and stepped into the corridor.

Everything was back to normal, but they still knew almost nothing.

Kunsan Air Base

Gunsan-si, South Korea

Dawson stepped off the US Air Force-owned Cessna Citation X+, the fastest business jet in the world. It had put them in South Korea far faster than a Herc, and all the equipment they would need beyond their personal weapons and gear would be provisioned from stores kept at Kunsan Air Base.

A Humvee pulled up and a lieutenant colonel climbed out. They all saluted and the man returned it.

He addressed Dawson. "Welcome to South Korea, Sergeant Major." He pointed toward a Black Hawk helicopter, its rotors already spinning. "Your transport is ready." He handed over a sealed envelope. "Secure communique from your CO. Apparently, things have changed."

"Thank you, sir," replied Dawson as he handed the envelope over to his second in command, Master Sergeant Mike "Red" Belme, who tore into it. "Our equipment?"

"Everything you asked for is sitting in front of that chopper, waiting to be inspected."

Dawson turned to the others and flicked a finger toward the pile. "Check it. We can't risk anything being missed. There's no chance of resupply once we're inserted."

The team sprinted toward the pile.

"And don't forget to make sure everything works!" It wasn't unheard of for an item to come off a shelf and be put into operation only for the poor bastard who needed it to discover the night vision goggles or whatever the hell it was didn't function. And in a combat situation, or a situation like they were about to find themselves in, deep inside enemy lines, you were hooped.

Red stepped over and whispered in his ear. "They changed course."

Dawson frowned. It meant less time to get prepared. "Understood. Looks like the shit's hitting the fan a little bit earlier than expected, sir."

The colonel laughed. "That's what I figured, which is why I had your bird prepped." He extended a hand. "Good hunting, Sergeant Major."

"Thank you, sir." Dawson shook the man's hand then he and Red joined the team. "Report."

Atlas stood nearby with an electronic checklist. "Everything's here, Sergeant Major, and everything appears to be functional."

"Appears?"

Atlas shrugged. "I doubt they want us firing off an eighty-four here just to make sure it works."

Dawson chuckled. "I suppose not. Okay, let's get it all in the bird."

The equipment was loaded and within minutes of landing, they were taking off once again. And if all went according to plan, they would be inside North Korea within an hour. Unfortunately, it meant their insertion would be hurried, which was when mistakes could happen.

And mistakes got people killed.

Director Morrison's Office, CIA Headquarters
Langley, Virginia

Leroux entered Morrison's office and found the man on the phone. The Chief held up a finger then pointed at a chair. Leroux sat and listened to the one-sided conversation, the Chief mostly saying, "Yeah" repeatedly.

"Okay, keep me posted." Morrison hung up the phone then pointed at it. "Delta just landed in South Korea. They've already been redeployed for their insertion."

"Will they be able to get into position in time?"

"It'll be tight. Luckily, their destination is close to the coast and we had a successful equipment insertion made overnight. Assuming they can make it inland undetected, then they should be able to get into position. But with everything that's happening, the kill order has now been extended to include Burkett."

Leroux tensed. "But, sir—"

Morrison cut him off. "Both Kane and Burkett are to be eliminated at the first opportunity. The order comes directly from the president."

Leroux sighed. "Any chance of reprieve on that?"

"No. Unless we come up with some evidence that proves beyond a doubt that something else is going on here, Dylan Kane and Dr. Burkett will be dead before the day is out."

"Well, I don't know what that evidence is going to be, though I've just eliminated my team as possible sources for the mole."

Morrison's eyebrows rose. "How so?"

"I signed out a scanner from the quartermaster. When you received that message a few minutes ago, I was able to confirm that the relay signal was not sent from anyone in the operations center, though it was sent from someone in this building."

Morrison grunted. "Well, that's something, at least. And considering how few people actually know what's going on, it reduces the possibilities dramatically."

"What did the message say?"

Morrison brought it up on his phone then pushed it across his desk. Leroux rose and took it, reading the message aloud.

"The future is looking bright in my new home. Don't do anything rash now." He put the phone back on Morrison's desk. "What do you think it means?"

Morrison shook his head. "I haven't had much time to think about it. He's obviously referring to Burkett being delivered safely, but I'm not sure what he means by 'don't do anything rash now.'"

Leroux scratched his chin. "Everything he's sent has been very deliberate. From what we can tell, he's been planning this for at least weeks, so we have to assume the messages were well thought out. Extremely well thought out, if you think about it. Whoever is triggering these messages could have been given a hundred different choices based upon different scenarios, but instead, there are only twelve messages in that system, seven of which have now been sent. And the last message we know goes to Fang. That leaves only four more messages. They could be contingency messages for different scenarios, but I have a funny feeling they're not, because every single one of them has been triggered in the order they were recorded in the system. It's as if he knew every step of his plan would succeed."

Morrison leaned back and folded his arms. "That's the exact type of cockiness I would expect from him, however, there is another explanation."

"What's that?"

"That if the plan failed at any point, contingency messaging wouldn't matter because he'd be dead, and that final message to Fang could be the key to explaining what the hell's going on."

Leroux agreed. "That makes sense. If his defection hadn't been successful, the North Koreans would've just shot him or tortured him to death. If the kidnapping of Burkett had failed, then they would've blamed him and done the same. Then if we had shot Burkett down, it would've proven that anything he could do for them was useless, so again, they eliminate him. The question is, what does this message mean? Everything sent to you has served a purpose."

Morrison picked up the phone. "'Don't do anything rash now.' I think the key here is the word 'rash.' So, what does rash mean?"

Leroux shrugged. "My middle name isn't Webster, but I've always thought it meant, don't do anything impulsively."

"That's how I would interpret it as well. So, rashness would imply that because they have Burkett, we would act rashly by trying to eliminate him now that he's on the ground, and eliminate Kane now that he's proven he's a traitor by giving the North Koreans an extremely valuable asset."

"That's how I'd interpret it. And if the president has already given the kill order for both of them, there's your rash act. Sir, we need to stop that order. I think there's something more going on here and Kane's just given us the signal that he needs more time."

Morrison raised a finger. "Or he's trying to confuse us so that we don't kill him, and it gives him time to get Burkett safely in place and himself safely hidden away somewhere that we can't get at him."

Leroux slammed his fists against the arms of his chair. "This is all so frustrating. What the hell is going on? This is what I don't get. Him and I are best friends. If there's anyone that could help him with this, it would be me, so why wouldn't he have told me if he was up to something? The fact that he didn't tell me, didn't tell Fang, didn't tell anyone that he trusts, just makes it look like he actually did defect."

"Maybe he has," said Morrison. "Every action he's taken so far, every message sent, every action taken by the North Koreans suggests he actually has defected. And unfortunately, the president is right.

Absent some other piece of information, the correct order is to eliminate them both."

Leroux rose. "Then I better get back at it and see if I can find that piece of information."

"Just remember, your team are only observers for the Delta op. Epps' team is going to be handling the takedown."

"Understood, sir." Leroux stepped out of the office and headed for the elevators, physically ill. He made a beeline for the bathrooms and vomited. His best friend was about to die, and he could see no way to stop it.

Sunchon Airbase

Sunchon, North Korea

Choe exchanged relieved handshakes with the rest of the team as the plane's tires chirped and the engines reversed, signaling a successful end to the mission. Yet would it be considered a success? The Americans had intercepted them and threatened to shoot them down, which meant they knew who had taken Burkett. The question that he didn't have an answer to was whether this was a concern to Command. If it wasn't, and their only concern was getting their hands on this scientist, then the mission was indeed a success. But if they had wanted it executed with the Americans never knowing who had taken him, it was an abject failure.

Yet, he had to assume Command didn't care, because the plan all along had been to change their course at the last minute and never land in China. If they had wanted to hide the fact his country was involved, they would have had them land in China, just as the flight plan indicated, then they could have disappeared within its 1.4 billion people and made their way securely across the border, even if the Americans had eventually figured out what plane they were on. They never would have proven this was a North Korean operation.

But now there was no doubt, and tricking them had never been the plan. Why was far above his level of responsibility, but he had to assume there was a reason behind it. It could be that the leadership feared the Chinese might want Burkett for themselves if they found him on their soil, but he suspected it was something far less sinister. It was a slap in the face to the imperial dogs that thought they were so superior. His country had taken one of the Americans' top scientists and gotten away with it, and boldly landing here was the ultimate insult.

The plane taxied toward one of the hangars and they rolled to a stop inside. The engines quieted as the massive doors shut, hiding them from any prying eyes. At any given time, he had no doubt there was an American spy satellite staring down at every square inch of North Korean territory, which was why so many of their procedures were designed to be done out of sight.

One of the flight crew opened the door to the plane and pushed out the stairs. Choe pointed at Burkett. "Remain seated."

Burkett stared out the window and shrugged. "Not much to see regardless."

Again with the attitude. Part of him wished he had received orders to kill the man, but if Burkett could help his country move forward, a little attitude was worth it. A steady power supply. It was something he could only imagine before being assigned to the United States. There he hadn't lost power once, and had only experienced a few bumps, all during major storms. To think that his country, thanks to what his team had accomplished, could experience constant uninterrupted power was exciting.

A colonel and his minions emerged from a door on the port side of the aircraft. Choe stepped down the stairs and onto the concrete floor. He was in civilian attire, but snapped out a salute regardless.

It was returned.

"How would you characterize the mission, Major?"

"A success, sir. We extracted the asset without any local interference and without injury, and have successfully delivered him to the motherland."

"Yet you were almost shot out of the sky."

"But we weren't. The Americans didn't have the courage to act."

"Your incompetence gave you away."

Choe chose his words carefully. "There were few options available to us. Command wanted him here now, so that meant an immediate extraction by air. If we had been given another day to plan, the Americans would have never known."

"So, it's Command's fault."

Choe's stomach flipped. Something was going on here. He should have received a hero's welcome, but instead he was getting grilled for no reason. "I'm sorry, Colonel, but there's nothing to blame Command for. Our original orders were to change course at the last minute and deviate from our filed flight plan. Since those orders were issued by

Command, they clearly weren't concerned if it was discovered that we were behind the abduction."

The colonel grunted and smiled slightly. "You're quick on your feet, Major, a skill you just might need for your next assignment."

Choe hid his disappointment. "I thought I was going to get to see my family, sir."

"All in good time, Major. At the moment, we have another assignment for you."

"And what's that?"

"We have a new asset that could prove extremely valuable. He's an American defector."

Choe jerked his chin back toward the aircraft. "You mean the one who supplied us this guy's name?"

"Yes. Command wants to keep him happy, so they're going to loosen the leash on him slightly. We want your team to keep an eye on him from a distance. See if he does anything unusual. But more importantly, keep him alive."

Choe's eyes narrowed. "Keep him alive?"

"We have reason to believe the Americans will attempt to take him out before he can provide us with any more names."

"Why not just lock him up in some place with no windows?"

The colonel shook his head. "That's not the deal he negotiated. And like I said, Command wants to keep him *extremely* happy." He pointed at the aircraft. "Apparently, he can provide us with as many of those guys as we want in any area of expertise. This could be the biggest intelligence coup in the history of our nation. The longer we keep him alive and happy, the more of these people we can bring in." He indicated the door he had come through. "Bring the prisoner inside. He'll be debriefed then transferred to his new handlers. Your team will be brought to Pyongyang immediately."

"Understood, sir."

The colonel regarded him for a moment. "When's the last time you saw your family?"

"Three years, sir."

"And your men?"

"I never met them before today, but similar, I'm sure."

"Very well. I'll arrange to have all your families meet you before you go out on assignment again. Just for a few minutes, mind you. Your mission is far more important than a family reunion."

Choe beamed a smile at the colonel and his unexpected kindness. "Thank you, sir. You have no idea how much that means to me, and to my men, I'm sure."

The colonel smirked. "Don't let it get around that I'm a nice guy. It could affect my reputation."

Choe laughed. "As far as anyone's concerned including myself, I'm still terrified of you."

The colonel tapped Choe's chest. "As you should be."

South of Yung-ni

North Korean Coast

Dawson's visor cleared the water but he remained submerged. He slowly scanned from left to right, confirming what Control had already said. They were clear. Two different satellites were providing coverage and drones had been deployed from the submarine used to insert them just offshore. He pushed to his feet, exposing himself to anyone who might be monitoring the shore, but no one opened fire, no one shouted a warning.

And Control remained silent in his ear.

He advanced forward as the others emerged from the water behind him. He rushed across the rocky beach toward the tree line then quickly stripped out of his wet gear as the other five handpicked for the mission joined him. Red and the other half of the team remained on board the sub in case they needed to be inserted later, but if they were, it meant something had gone horribly wrong.

He checked his gear and weapons as the others hid their wet gear, then activated his comms. "Control, Bravo Zero-One. We're secure at point Alpha, proceeding to point Bravo, over."

"Copy that, Zero-One. Still no indication they've detected you, over."

"Copy that, Control. Zero-One, out." He turned to the others. "Let's get a wiggle on, ladies. I want to be out of here as soon as possible with only the holes I arrived here with."

Niner grinned. "Don't you worry, BD. When we're back on the sub, I'll check everyone over to make sure your loved ones aren't in for any surprises."

Atlas groaned as they pushed through the trees. "The sad thing is that I don't think he's joking."

"Don't you worry, big guy. I'll check you over twice just so you don't get jealous."

Atlas shoved Niner into a tree, resulting in snickers.

Dawson hissed at them. "Pipe down! The forest could have ears."

Everyone zipped their mouth shut and they continued forward, Dawson's tactical computer guiding them to point Bravo where they had been assured their special equipment was waiting undiscovered by the North Koreans. In less than ten minutes, they were at the small clearing.

"There!" said Atlas, pointing at the trees ahead where several parachute canopies were caught in the branches. In plain sight. The only reason the computer-guided drop hadn't been discovered was that nobody apparently patrolled this area.

Dawson indicated for Atlas, Niner, Jagger, and Spock to establish a perimeter while he and Jimmy pulled down the chutes.

"Control, Zero-One, we're at point Bravo. Confirm area is secure, over."

"Affirmative, Zero-One. We show no hostiles in your area. Just a reminder, you have a road less than a klick from your location that for the moment is clear."

"Copy that, Control. Zero-One, out." He turned to the others. "Atlas, Niner, give us a hand. Spock and Jagger, maintain watch."

Atlas emerged from the trees with Niner, and the four of them set to work on uncrating then assembling their special delivery—six electric motorcycles, whisper-quiet with run-flat tires and bullet-resistant glass and casings. Both on and off-road capable. These would hopefully get them to where they needed to be on time, then out of any situation they might create. They had all ridden them in training, and they were a blast. But training was one thing. This was real life, and he had no doubt things were about to get nasty.

Within minutes, they had six of the motorcycles assembled and a forty-mile journey ahead of them that they could easily do in half an hour if they took the roads. But that might not be possible. He straddled his bike and flicked the switch, turning on the motor. Silent. It was impressive. Bikers who loved the throaty roar of a hog would absolutely hate these machines, and it reminded him of how every time he was in an electric car, he missed the purr of his Mustang's engine and the growl when he gave it some gas. But everything had its purpose, and while he might prefer to be riding a vintage Victory

163

bagger with custom ape hangers into battle because it might look cool for when they made a movie of his life, it would also be heard from a mile away.

He looked at the others, everyone now on their assigned bike, a mix of MP5s and M4s mounted in their cradles. "Control, Zero-One, we're ready to proceed. What's the status on that road, over?"

"Zero-One, Control, we have two military vehicles approaching from the coast, but it's clear ahead of them for at least five klicks. No evidence of roadblocks or cameras. If you go now, you'll get ahead of them and should have no problem keeping ahead, over."

"Copy that, Control. Heading for the road now." He turned to the others. "Let's go, gentlemen. We don't want to get caught in traffic." He gunned the throttle and jerked forward far too rapidly due to the incredible torque from the electric motor. He eased off slightly, preferring not to be impaled by a low-hanging branch, then guided them through the trees, the underbrush fortunately light.

He spotted the road ahead. "Control, Zero-One, report."

"You're still good if you go now," was the immediate reply.

He cranked the throttle and his bike leaped forward, and moments later he was making a hard left onto the road. He did a shoulder check to make sure the rest of the team was still with him, then gunned it. "Control, Zero-One, we're on the road. Keep me updated on any changes with the hostiles behind us and anything ahead of us. At these speeds, we're going to come up on stuff fast, over."

"Copy that, Zero-One. Hostiles behind you are now two klicks back and you're rapidly opening the gap. There's still no sign of anything in front of you. We'll warn you of anything the moment we see it, over."

Dawson leaned forward then checked his tactical computer. The kidnapped scientist was already on the ground and they had no idea where Kane was. Right now, the mission was to get as close to the scientist as possible with the hopes that Kane would be brought out to meet the man whose life he had effectively ended.

Dawson still couldn't believe the mission. Kane was a friend, a brother in arms, and he couldn't believe that the man would betray his country like this. But then again, he had seen men and women he had respected for years go crazy over the past four, believing in conspiracy theories that any sane person should know were complete and utter bullshit.

Could Kane have fallen victim? He couldn't see how. Typically, those that believed the craziness got most of their information from social media or other dark corners on the net. Kane wouldn't have time for such nonsense, and even if he did, he understood how the algorithms worked because covert ops used those same algorithms to manipulate what people saw. A binary society was what Professor James Acton called it, and the man was right. The problem here, though, was there was no way he could believe that Kane had fallen victim to it. Yet unless someone found proof that he was up to something good, their orders still stood.

Kill him on sight.

And the fact the voices in his ear were not from Leroux's team told him the powers that be back home weren't taking any chances. They wanted the orders executed.

Somebody stepped from the trees, decked out in full camouflage, and raised a weapon. Dawson cursed as he reached forward and shifted the aim of his mounted MP5. He squeezed the trigger as he gently applied the brakes. This wasn't a matter of getting past the hostile by causing him to hit the ground—they had to eliminate him so he couldn't report back. The burst of lead from his weapon was joined by two more behind him, and before the hostile could get a shot off, his body was shaking with the impacts.

Dawson squeezed the brakes hard, bringing him to a rapid stop. He leaped off the bike and rushed into the trees, taking a knee behind a large trunk as the others did the same, scattering across both sides of the road. He listened as he steadied his pounding heart, then adjusted toward the crashing sounds of someone approaching. His trained ear told him it was one person. He drew his Glock and quickly twisted the suppressor in place just as a North Korean regular appeared. Dawson put two in the chest, dropping the man, then advanced and put two more in the man's head.

He took a knee again, cocking an ear, but heard no one else. He activated his comms. "Bravo Team, Zero-One. Anybody hearing any hostiles, over?"

A string of negatives replied.

"Control, Zero-One, we were forced to take out two hostiles that were in the trees. Status on hostiles behind us, over."

"Copy that, Zero-One. We just watched the engagement. Hostiles are rapidly approaching. You have two minutes before they're on top of you."

"Copy that." Dawson sprang to his feet, heading back to the road. "Hide that body and let's go."

Atlas and Niner grabbed the first hostile and hauled him into the tree line and out of sight as Dawson climbed on his bike and waited for the others.

"Zero-One, Control, they'll be coming around the bend in thirty seconds, over."

"Copy that."

Atlas climbed on his bike, the shocks protesting, and he gave a thumbs-up. Dawson cranked the throttle and all six of them were underway again.

"Twenty seconds. You need to get around the next bend otherwise you're in plain sight."

"No shit," he muttered, the throttle fully cranked. The bend was just ahead. All they had to do was round it and they'd be out of sight.

"Ten seconds."

He was going to make it. The question was, would they all make it? While the two men they had just killed had no radios on them, they would eventually be missed. But those in the vehicles would definitely have radios and would call in six men on motorcycles that belonged in a science fiction movie. It would blow the op. The two dead soldiers were a problem, but at the moment, they were a problem without an explanation. The North Koreans would have no doubt they had been killed by hostile armed forces, and would likely assume it was related to Kane's defection and the kidnapping of Burkett. But they would also have no idea as to numbers and location, and if they were lucky, his team would have already completed the mission before the soldiers were discovered missing.

He leaned to his left, taking the bend at full throttle before killing any of his speed. He struggled to maintain control, his front wheel wobbling for a few moments of terror before he regained his balance and straightened out, accelerating again. He checked his mirrors and breathed a relieved sigh to see the others had successfully navigated the sharp turn. "Control, Zero-One, report!"

"Zero-One, Control. It looks like you just made it. No evidence that they saw you, over."

"Copy that, Control. Keep an eye on them. Let us know if they spot the two hostiles we just took out, over." Dawson took the next bend in the road a little slower this time, and as he confirmed Atlas, taking up the rear, had also cleared it, he breathed a little easier and relaxed his grip on the throttle slightly. At the speeds they were doing, they should reopen the gap easily.

"Zero-One, Control. Your two hostiles have cleared the incident area. It looks like you're home free for now. The road is still clear ahead of you, however there could still be hostiles in the trees, over."

"Copy that, Control. Keep watching our six and the road ahead, and find out where the hell our target is. This entire region's going to be crawling the moment those two don't report in."

"We're working on it, Zero-One."

Dawson didn't bother responding. There was no point. He had no doubt everyone was doing everything they could to find Kane so this mission could be a success. He would just feel better if it were Leroux's team on the other end of the comms, because in his entire career, they were by far the best he had worked with.

Pothong Riverside Terraced Residential District

Pyongyang, North Korea

Kane climbed into the Pyeonghwa Zunma after Kwan, the basic vehicle apparently the North Korean equivalent to a luxury sedan for VIPs. To their credit, the car was spotless and appeared well-maintained. Major Pak smiled at him then glanced at Kwan. "I trust you had a good night?"

Kane grinned. "Excellent night."

Kwan giggled and took his hand. "Perfect night."

"I'm happy to hear that. And you'll be happy to hear that Dr. Burkett is safely on the ground on North Korean territory."

"That's great news," said Kane. "I trust he's cooperating?"

"I'm not sure that's how I would characterize it. Your briefing on him seems to have been quite accurate—an arrogant self-absorbed man who thinks he's been put on this earth to singlehandedly solve mankind's problems, and doesn't care who he's working for. He's being debriefed right now, and the initial report is that he's basically told everyone in the room to piss off and let him get to work."

Kane chuckled. "That sounds like him, all right. And are you going to let him go to work?"

"At the moment, we see no reason why not. He'll be supervised closely, obviously, but Command is eager to get him working so that we can get our nuclear power plant online before the end of the year."

"If anybody can do it, he can. We had a power outage last night for over an hour. Is that normal?"

Pak nodded. "I'm afraid it is, thanks to your country's sanctions."

Kane raised a finger. "My former country."

Pak bowed his head. "Your former country's sanctions. It's difficult to get the spare parts to repair our regular power plants. If we can get a working nuclear reactor design entirely built in North Korea, with North Korean and Russian parts, we could replicate them across the country and bring stable, bountiful power to the entire population."

"An essential first step to your country's future success. Idle factories can't produce goods, and darkened bedrooms don't let the next generation read."

"Well said." Pak glanced at Kwan then at Kane. "Should Burkett work out, I have a feeling you'll be able to ask for anything you want, and my country will happily provide it."

Kane put his arm around Kwan. "I've already got a big part of what I want. Thank you very much."

Kwan beamed a smile at him then kissed his cheek.

"But once you're satisfied, we'll have to discuss better quarters. While last night's were dramatically better than my first night, I think you can do better, though for now I'm content where I am. I'm not greedy. I would like, however, to discuss a little more freedom."

Pak shook his head. "It's far too early for that."

Kane batted a hand. "That's not what I mean. I'd like for Kwan and I to be able to go out for a walk, go to a restaurant, sit in the park rather than be confined to my apartment. You can, of course, have a guard on us at a discreet distance. I have no problem with that and I understand entirely. I'm just not used to being cooped up."

Pak regarded him for a moment before giving a curt nod. "I'll mention it to my superiors. I'm sure they'll approve it, as long as you have no contact with anyone."

Kane smiled. "Agreed, no contact with anyone. Kwan is all I need for now." He wagged a finger at Pak. "And I still think you and I are going to be friends eventually."

Pak laughed. "Are all you Americans like this?"

Kane squeezed Kwan tighter. "I hope not, otherwise I'm not as special as I think I am."

The driver said something that Kane pretended to not understand.

"What was that?"

Kwan lifted her head from his shoulder and whispered in his ear. "He said we're almost at the airport."

Kane stared out the window. "Excellent. I'm eager to meet Dr. Burkett."

Pak's eyebrows shot up. "Wait a minute. You've never met him before?"

"Of course not."

"But I thought you knew him?"

Kane shook his head. "No, I know *of* him. I was responsible for setting up security for him when he had traveled to a conference outside the country. Scientists and people like me don't exactly mix, but when we do, we get extensive dossiers, which is why I knew he was exactly what you were looking for, and it's why I know who you're looking for in countless specialties. Me knowing them is of no use, my knowing *of* them is everything. All you need to do is trust me and I'll get you everybody you need, and they'll be every bit as good in their field as Burkett is."

A frown creased Pak's face for a moment before it finally relaxed into a more neutral expression.

"Relax, Major. I promise I won't let you down. I realize we both have a lot riding on this, not the least of which is my life. I would not have come here if I couldn't fulfill every promise I made."

Pak grunted. "These are early days, Mr. Kane. Trust is built over time. Lies won't be tolerated nor will omission. The next time we speak, I expect you to be entirely truthful and forthcoming. I don't want anything implied."

"Agreed."

The vehicle came to a halt.

"Now, how about we go meet our scientist?"

Operations Center 2, CIA Headquarters

Langley, Virginia

"Holy shit! I've got eyes on Kane!" cried Child.

The entire operations center came to a halt, everyone turning toward the main displays. A satellite shot, taken from a slight angle due to its orbit, showed a black vehicle park outside the hangar they had been watching. Its occupants climbed out and what appeared to be a chauffeur in a military uniform stood by his door. An officer waited on the passenger side while a man and a woman in civilian attire on the driver's side rounded the rear of the vehicle.

Leroux peered at the civilian male. It was impossible to tell who it was. "What makes you say it's him?"

"Just wait for it. This is a replay from a few minutes ago."

The man wrapped an arm around the woman's shoulders and bile filled Leroux's mouth at the betrayal. If this were indeed Kane, he'd been there only two days and already had a woman, and with the situation what it was, the woman was no doubt a pro and Kane would have already taken advantage of what was freely on offer.

"Shit, man, that's pretty cold," muttered someone behind him.

Leroux shook his head. "Don't read too much into that. When he is on a mission, he has to play a part. Right now, we still don't know what's going on."

"Here it comes," said Child.

Everybody leaned toward the display and the man looked up at the sky, staring at the heavens for a solid two-count before walking toward the hangar and disappearing inside.

It was Kane.

Leroux collapsed back in his chair. There was no doubt that it was his friend, and the facial recognition software confirmed its findings, flashing the results on the massive screens.

Tong turned in her seat to face him. "What do we do now?"

"There's nothing we can do. Once Delta is in position, their orders are to take the shot unless we've found something that proves there's more going on here. All we've seen here is more evidence that he's guilty. He's at the site where Burkett was taken, and I see no evidence of handcuffs or heavy guard."

"Not to mention he's got a piece of ass on his arm already," commented Child.

"Tactlessly put, but correct. Everything here, like everything so far, can be interpreted in two ways. And like Marc said earlier, we have to err on the side of caution. If Delta can get there in time, I see no reason for them not to take the shot." He turned to Child. "Make sure Epps' team has that. They might have missed it."

"Yes, sir." Child tapped away at his terminal, sending the isolated footage and the facial recognition confirmation to the team controlling the operation. The fact Kane had been allowed in the open confirmed that the North Koreans had no idea the Delta team had been inserted. Hopefully, their ignorance would last long enough to put an end to this mission once and for all. Whatever Kane was up to was putting people's lives in danger. At the moment, that not only included the kidnapped scientist, but it also included the six Bravo Team members on the ground, plus the other six and the submarine crew waiting offshore. And that ignored what could happen if Burkett was allowed to continue his work and give the despotic regime unlimited power.

Kane and the others disappeared inside the hangar and Leroux pushed back from his station, hanging his head between his knees as his stomach churned and he fought the urge to vomit. His friend was about to die and there was nothing they could do about it, and he could find no reason that they should do something about it. All the evidence suggested he was guilty, and it was simply too dangerous to let him live. He pushed upright and stared at the screen. "Show me Delta's position with respect to that hangar."

Tong brought up a map showing the six-member team rapidly closing in on the area using back roads.

"ETA?"

Tong shrugged. "Depends on how close they want to get. Some of them are among the best shots in the world. Niner can probably take him out from over a mile with ease."

"What's the weather?"

Tong checked. "Sunny with blue skies, no measurable wind, temperature estimate is seventy-seven degrees with low humidity."

Leroux sighed. "Perfect sniper weather." He brought out his phone and sent an encrypted message to Sherrie.

Dylan has been found. Anticipate kill shot in the coming minutes. Tell Fang I'm so sorry, but I couldn't find anything to save him.

Kane's off-the-books Operations Center

Outside Bethesda, Maryland

Fang leaped to her feet as she read the message just sent to Sherrie by Leroux, her chair crashing into the wall. "Why?" she screamed in horror and sorrow. "Why did you do this? Why didn't you tell me?"

Sherrie approached her, her arms extended to embrace her, but Fang waved her off.

"No, don't touch me! Nobody touch me!" she snapped as her shoulders shook. "I don't want anybody to touch me ever again!" She folded her arms as a chill washed over her. "I have to get out of here."

She rushed down the corridor and opened the door to the outside. She slammed it shut behind her and ran blindly among the other containers and trailers, one minute sobbing uncontrollably, the next shouting in rage, her fist darting out and punching anything within reach.

None of this made sense. Why was he doing this? He wasn't a traitor. There was no way he could be a traitor. Something else had to be going on. There was just no way the man she loved would betray his country like this. But it didn't matter anymore what was really going on. It was too late, the orders had been given, the target had been found, and the team was almost in place. She understood the calculations involved. They might never get another chance to take him out. Even if he were innocent, there was no way they could risk leaving him alive in case he wasn't, and she didn't blame them.

She leaned against a container, sliding to the ground, and sat there for a few minutes before drying her eyes with a knuckle from each hand. He could be dead by now, and she gasped as she remembered there was a message due to be sent to her. If the mole inside the CIA was privy to his elimination, would they trigger that message to be sent early, or would she be tortured over the coming hours, left to wonder what final words her beloved had to say that would have to sustain her for the rest of her days?

She pushed to her feet and trudged back to the containers housing the operations center, dreading what news might await her.

Sunchon Airbase Perimeter

Sunchon, North Korea

Dawson propped his motorcycle against a tree then threw some camouflage netting over it as the others did the same around him. They'd be going on foot now, as there was a checkpoint ahead blocking their route to the airport. Unfortunately for the North Koreans, and perhaps more critically Kane, the airport wasn't far. They had four sniper rifles with them and a perimeter cleared of trees and any obstructions for a klick in all directions, intended to give the guards a clear view of anyone approaching—the security for the airport was all designed around either repelling an outright assault or preventing any covert infiltration.

His team wasn't there for an assault, nor were they there to sneak in. With all obstructions removed, it meant their job could be easily done from a kilometer out, which was exactly what they were going to do.

Dawson rushed through the trees with the others, everyone silent, all having previously expressed their dismay that Kane's presence had been confirmed. They all knew what the job was, and they would all carry it through. Yet nobody wanted to, and all would have preferred if Kane wasn't here so they could have failed at their mission and not killed their friend.

Niner jogged up beside him. "I'll take the shot."

Dawson glanced over at him. "Are you sure?"

Niner nodded, his expression somber, none of the usual joy in evidence. "I'm the best shot here. I can do it clean. He won't suffer. He deserves at least that, just in case we're wrong."

Dawson agreed, slapping Niner on the back. "You're a good man. I think he'd be honored to have the job done by you."

Niner chuckled. "He might be honored, but he'd probably be happier to have a piss-poor shot make the attempt and fail."

Dawson laughed. "You're probably right." He held up a fist as they approached the tree line then crouched, inching forward. "Control, Zero-One. We're at the tree line to the airport. Status report, over."

"Primary target is in a hangar marked Alpha Two. Secondary target was last seen entering the same hangar, over."

Dawson frowned. "Copy that, Control. I'm more concerned with the security. Any signs of patrols along the perimeter, over?"

"Affirmative, Zero-One. We have a single light armored vehicle circling the ring road, four men on board, going too fast to see anything useful. They're currently on the number three side of the airport, opposite your current position. Will advise when they approach. Note that we pulled back the drones. We can't risk them being spotted. We're on satellite-only now, over."

"Understood, Control. Just keep your eyes peeled for the targets and any patrols on foot hidden in the trees."

"We'll do our best, Zero-One."

Dawson peered through his binoculars, searching for anything suspicious up and down the road they now faced, but found nothing. He turned to Niner then froze. He was nowhere to be seen. Dawson dropped to a knee and scanned the area when a tree to his right giggled and Niner emerged in his ghillie suit.

"I still got it."

Dawson gave him a look. "You're lucky I didn't shoot you. When a tree giggles like a little girl, I usually put two rounds in it."

Atlas appeared in his own ghillie suit. "What, you don't like trees?"

Niner wagged a finger. "No, I think he doesn't like little girls."

Dawson gave them both the finger. "I don't like foliage that talks back. Now, you two ready?"

"Yup."

"Then find good nests. I have no idea how long we're going to be here and we can't have you repositioning every time a patrol drives by, understood?"

They both confirmed, then Niner and Atlas broke off with Jimmy and Spock as their spotters. Within minutes, Niner and Atlas were in elevated positions, their customized ghillie suits adapted specifically for the terrain they found themselves in, allowing them to blend into their surroundings.

"Zero-One, Control. Security patrol is nearing your position, over."

"Copy that, Control." He signaled to the others and everyone faded into the background as the engine of the approaching vehicle grew louder. It drove past their position doing at least thirty miles per hour, and from his vantage point, he could tell that nobody was paying close attention to the tree line and were instead focused on the road ahead or the cleared area around the airport. If this was the only security they'd have to deal with, this could prove to be a cakewalk, but unfortunately there were two dead bodies out there that somebody would be missing soon, which could see this place crawling with troops any minute now. For the sake of his team, he prayed Kane showed himself soon so they could take the shot and fall back to the submarine and safety. But part of him begged God to keep Kane inside so that they wouldn't have to shoot their friend.

It just might give Langley enough time to figure out what was really going on here.

Sunchon Airbase

Sunchon, North Korea

Pak watched as Kane shook Burkett's hand after the introductions had been made, paying close attention to everyone's mannerisms.

"That's quite the handshake you've got there," commented Kane with a smile. "Not something I'd expect out of a scientist."

Burkett shrugged. "My father taught me at a young age how to shake a hand properly. I've found that with people like you who don't understand just how much more important I am than they are, a firm, confident handshake seems to at least suggest I'm their equal. Some weak, limp-wristed handshake that many of my colleagues give because they're intimidated by all those around them, simply contributes toward the alphas of our culture believing they're superior merely because they're physically strong. The meek shall inherit the earth is just a line. It's the intelligent who will eventually rule this world."

Kane regarded the man with a bemused expression. "Rule?"

Burkett shrugged. "For the lack of a better word. Control, guide, govern, however you want to look at it, the era when the strong rule the weak is coming to an end."

Kane chuckled and turned to Pak. "Isn't he exactly how I described?" Kane returned his attention to the kidnapped scientist. "While I think the world would be a better place should it be ruled by science rather than tyranny, just remember, strong men and women are required until the enemy is no more, because most of the tyrants of the world don't yet subscribe to your philosophy."

Burkett bowed his head slightly. "Agreed on all points." He turned to Pak and waved a hand at the other North Koreans in the room. "They've told me almost nothing. Why am I here?"

"You are here to benefit the people of North Korea."

"That doesn't concern me. That's politics. I'm concerned with science. So, I'll ask again, why am I here?"

Pak bristled at the utter lack of respect shown. The extraction team's assessment of the man and what Kane had said were certainly accurate. This was an unparalleled level of arrogance and he hoped it meant Burkett knew he was as good as they thought, and was confident he could get away with anything because he was too valuable to them. "Very well, Dr. Burkett. We have a nuclear power program that has been stalled since the sixties. You've been brought in to fix what's wrong and provide us with stable, uninterrupted power."

Burkett smiled slightly. "I'm well aware of your failed program. It can be fixed quite easily."

Eyebrows throughout the room shot up.

"How?" asked Pak.

"It's really quite simple. The mistake you've made is putting your trust in the Russians. While they may be your allies, they're not your friends. The nuclear reactor you built is based upon specs provided by them. All the advisors you've brought in have been Russian and all they do is confirm that you've implemented the specs correctly. What you haven't been told, and what very few on this planet know, is that those specs are incorrect. Intentionally incorrect. The Russians don't want you to have nuclear power. They don't trust you. They've been actively sabotaging your nuclear program for decades, and the master stroke was the specifications they provided to you for that extremely expensive nuclear reactor you've got sitting in Nyongbyon that you just can't seem to bring online."

Pak's pulse pounded in his ears at the implications. Was Russia actually their enemy? For decades, they had told them to trust nobody but a North Korean, and it would appear their leaders had been right to think so. He calmed himself. "And you know what the error in the specifications is?"

"Of course I do. We had somebody on the inside years ago provide them to us, and one of my tasks was to determine what the problem was."

"And you figured it out?"

"Of course I figured it out."

"How?"

Burkett shrugged. "By being me. For years none of your scientists have been able to figure it out, though I suspect a lot of that is simply because they weren't looking. They trusted the Russian specs and the Russian advisors. This is why I rely on the science and leave the politics out of things. Trusting the source because they're a political ally is idiocy when it comes to science. Trust the science, and you can never go wrong."

"Is it an easy fix?"

Burkett tilted his head to the side and shrugged his shoulders. "On paper, I can fix it in five minutes, but it'll require a change to the design of your reactor. Under my supervision and with the proper resources, I suspect we would be ready for initial test runs before the end of the year. Ninety-nine percent of what you have is perfectly fine. This isn't a tear-down and redesign prospect. This is merely an exercise in correcting the flaw that was in the original specifications. Your people will have stable power by this time next year if your government is smart enough to let me get the job done."

A man entered the room and Pak snapped to attention despite the lack of a uniform. It was Doctor Ri Kyong-thaek, a renowned scientist and the head of their entire nuclear program, both civilian and military.

Ri stood in front of Burkett, ignoring everyone else. "I am Doctor Ri. Are you aware of who I am?"

Burkett shook his head. "Should I be?"

Ri frowned. "With your level of arrogance, I'd be surprised if you're even aware of the names of your colleagues. It doesn't matter though. Tell me what the flaw is."

Burkett ignored him and instead turned to Kane. "Since you're the only non-Korean in the room, I assume I have you to thank for my current predicament?"

Kane bowed slightly. "I'm afraid so."

"And why have you done this?"

"For entirely self-motivated, political reasons."

Burkett regarded him for a moment. "You mean the growing instability of our country and the inevitable collapse of the Western liberal democracy?"

"Exactly."

Pak hid his shock. Here was a scientist completely disconnected from the society within which he lived, and an intelligence operative from that same society who should be fully aware of everything going on within his country and around the world, both agreeing with what was going on in their home country. Could it be true? Kane had explained his motivations quite convincingly, however delusions were still delusions, and he didn't mind that, as long as it worked to his country's advantage. One delusional conspiracy theorist's shared intelligence was just as good as a sane man's if it were accurate. But if Burkett shared in the delusion, perhaps it wasn't a delusion after all.

Burkett turned to Pak. "You're in charge here?"

"I'm the senior ranking officer in the room," was all Pak was willing to admit since he wasn't certain how Dr. Ri felt about the hierarchy within these four walls.

Burkett pointed at Kane. "I want him with me at all times."

"To hell with that!" exclaimed Kane. "That was never part of the deal!"

Burkett shook his head. "I want a familiar face."

Pak frowned. "You mean a white face."

"No, I'm not a racist. I need somebody from back home that I can speak to who shares a common culture."

Kane waved his hands. "Hell no, Major. We have an agreement. I deliver him to you and I get my nice little life here. Find someone else."

Burkett rolled his eyes at Kane. "And just who would you have them get? It's not like this place is crawling with Americans."

Ri cleared his throat. "There is another."

Pak's eyebrows shot up but he said nothing.

"Who?" asked Burkett.

"Dr. Gorman. He's one of yours."

Burkett stared at the man. "Gorman? As in Dr. Nathan Gorman?"

"Exactly."

"Bullshit. He retired two months ago. He went completely off the grid. Nobody's heard from him since."

"That's the cover story your government gave, yes. We *liberated* him from his miserable retirement and brought him here to work on our reactor."

Burkett threw up his hands. "Then why did you need me? He should be able to figure out what's wrong."

"That's what we assumed as well, however he hasn't been very cooperative, which is why four weeks ago, operatives in the United States took his daughter and granddaughter into custody. He's now proving quite cooperative, even without you we would have our nuclear program back on track soon. With your assistance, we'll shave another year or two off of that."

Burkett smiled. "This is fantastic news. Gorman is an excellent scientist, not my caliber of course, but excellent nonetheless. It'll be a pleasure to work with him." He wagged a finger at Kane. "But I still want him with me. Gorman is an old man from a different generation. This one will be better company."

Pak glanced at Ri who gave a slight nod. "Very well, Dr. Burkett, Mr. Kane will accompany you—"

Kane glared at him. "No fu—"

Pak cut him off. "For the next several days to make your transition easier."

Kane relaxed slightly. "Fine. A few days, but she comes with me," he said, taking Kwan's hand.

She snuggled closer to him and Burkett raised a finger.

"Umm, can I get one of those?"

Operations Center 2, CIA Headquarters

Langley, Virginia

Leroux was going batshit crazy waiting. It was bad enough running an op where there were long stretches with nothing happening, but merely being an observer, with the op run from an entirely different operations center, was excruciating. He leaped to his feet then paced behind his station. Nobody said anything, but they all felt the same way. Everyone desperately wanted something to happen just to break the tension, but they were all acutely aware that when that something did happen, Dylan Kane would most likely die.

Delta was in position. There was no evidence so far that their presence in North Korea had been detected, and the drone left behind to monitor the area where the two soldiers had been taken out suggested their discovery wasn't coming anytime soon.

This could be a clean mission for a change. Go in, do your business, get out.

He frowned.

Tong looked up at him. "What?"

He flinched. "Huh?"

"You've got that look on your face."

He thought for a moment then chuckled. "I was just thinking that this op looks like it's going to go smoothly."

She laughed. "And you're wondering why ours never do?"

He tossed up his hands. "Exactly. Aren't we supposed to be the best?"

"We are!" shouted Therrien from the back of the room. "That's why they always throw the Charlie-Foxtrots at us. No way Epps' crew could handle those."

Cheers and claps of agreement filled the room, relieving some tension, when somebody brought them back to reality.

"We've got movement!"

The laughter stopped and everyone focused on the main displays. A side door to the hangar opened. Several soldiers emerged first, then Kane and his new woman, hand in hand, stepped into the late afternoon sunlight. Another man followed, and from the angle, he appeared Caucasian.

Leroux pointed. "Zoom in on him. That must be Burkett."

Tong tapped at her keyboard and a new window appeared showing a zoomed-in image of the cluster of people. Kane and the woman approached the vehicle they had arrived in, along with what was likely the officer that had brought them there. Another vehicle pulled up and the second cluster headed for it.

"Control, One-One, I have the shot. Am I cleared to take it, over?" came Niner's voice over the comms, broadcast on the overhead speakers.

"Affirmative, One-One. You are cleared to take the shot. I repeat, you are cleared to take the shot, over."

"Confirmation acknowledged. Awaiting Zero-Seven's acquisition of secondary target, over."

"Stand by," replied Atlas.

Leroux collapsed in his chair, not sure he wanted to see what was about to happen, yet unable to tear his eyes away from the final moments of his best friend's life.

And that was when Burkett stared up at the sky and everyone in the room, including Leroux, gasped in shock. Leroux grabbed his headset and fit it in place. "This is Leroux! Abort! Abort! Abort!" he shouted as Atlas' voice came in over the speakers.

"Secondary target acquired. Preparing to take the shot."

Leroux spun to Tong. "Am I on?"

She shook her head. "No, it looks like they've cut us out of the loop."

He cursed and tore the headset off, whipping the useless piece of shit across his station as he sprinted for the doors, pointing at Tong. "Call the Chief! We have to stop this!"

She reached for her phone as Leroux pushed against the heavy door sealing them inside. It opened enough for him to squeeze through and he sprinted down the corridor toward the operations center run by Epps.

Two guards stood on either side of the door.

"I need to get inside," he gasped as he reached for the panel.

One of them blocked him. "I'm sorry, sir. We have specific orders that no one from your team is allowed inside."

Leroux cursed. "You don't understand. They're about to kill an innocent man. We just identified the secondary target. It's not who we've been told it is. We have to stop this now. Just let me inside. You can shoot me later."

"I'm sorry, sir. We have our orders."

Leroux cursed. "Said countless men throughout history before unnecessary tragedies that could have been prevented were allowed to occur." He hauled out his phone and dialed the Chief. So much time had passed, he had little doubt Niner had already executed his orders and Kane was dead. He had known all along his best friend was innocent. There was no way he was a traitor.

And unfortunately, the proof had come too late.

Dr. Burkett wasn't Dr. Burkett at all.

He was another operations officer that they were well acquainted with.

Jack.

Just Jack.

Sunchon Airbase Perimeter

Sunchon, North Korea

Niner said a silent prayer for his aim to be true and for his friend, now in his sights, to die painlessly. He moved his finger from the trigger guard to the trigger, gently exhaling as he prepared to squeeze.

"Hold your fire!" hissed Atlas, and Niner moved his hand away but kept Kane in his scope.

Dawson's voice came over his headset. "Zero-Seven, explain."

"Zero-One, check the secondary target. Am I high or is that who I think it is?"

Niner desperately wanted to adjust his aim and see who the hell Atlas thought he saw, but that wasn't his mission. His mission was to kill Kane, and though Atlas had ordered him to stop, it wasn't Atlas' place to give that order. Only Dawson or Control could do that. He put his finger back on the trigger guard and prepared once again to take the shot, but stood by, for Kane was still standing outside the vehicle, and for the moment, it appeared there would be at least several more seconds in which to take him down cleanly.

Dawson cursed. "Holy shit! Okay, what the hell does that mean?"

Niner slowly adjusted his aim as Kane rounded the vehicle. "Would somebody care to explain what the hell is going on?"

"Stand by, One-One," replied Dawson from his vantage point ten yards to the left. "It appears that Burkett is actually Jack."

Niner's eyes narrowed. "Jack? As in Jack, the man with no last name?"

"Exactly."

"What the hell is he doing here?"

"Control, Zero-One, we're aborting. The secondary target is not Burkett. It's one of your operatives."

"Stand by, Zero-One, we're trying to find out what's going on here."

"Everybody hold your fire," said Dawson. "But keep your targets in sight. This still goes down if we receive the order."

Niner growled. "This is bullshit. We've been looking for that piece of evidence that something's going on, and if this isn't it, I don't know what the hell is. There's no way two of them defected. And I've met Jack. He's no nuclear physicist. So, unless that's his twin, he's undercover and Kane's defection was all just a ploy to get him inside."

Atlas backed him up. "He's right. Control, get your shit together. You know this isn't right."

"Maintain radio discipline, Bravo Team," snapped Dawson. "I give the order, no one else. Understood?"

"Understood," replied Niner as the others did the same. There was no way he was shooting Kane if some anonymous voice from Langley told him to. If Dawson did, he'd take the shot, no matter how hard it would be to do so, especially now, knowing something else was going on. The comms crackled in Niner's ear and the decision came down from above.

"Bravo Team, Control Actual. Abort! Abort! Abort! I repeat, abort the op! Stand by at your current position for further instructions."

Niner removed his right hand from his weapon and finally took the opportunity to adjust his aim to see the so-called Burkett as he acknowledged the order. "This is One-One, acknowledging abort, over."

Atlas did the same, the two active shooters acknowledging before Dawson did for the team as a whole. Niner shook his head as he found Jack in his scope.

What the hell are you two up to?

Operations Center 4, CIA Headquarters

Langley, Virginia

The door to the operations center hissed open and one of Epps' people emerged, her eyes bulging at finding Leroux standing there in a shouting match with the guards.

"Chris, Epps just sent me to get you. Something's happened."

"Please tell me you didn't take the shot."

She shook her head. "No." She beckoned him inside. "Come on, he wants to talk to you."

Leroux gave both guards a look as they stepped aside and he entered the operations center manned by Epps' team. He headed for the center of the room, his eyes glued to the displays, displays that showed Kane and the others alive and now climbing into their vehicles. "I assume you figured it out."

Epps shook his head. "Don't give us the credit. I gave the order to shoot, but one of the Delta team recognized Jack before we did. I've only worked with him a couple of times and had never actually seen his face."

Leroux's shoulders relaxed. "So, we're agreed?"

"Yes. I've already given the abort order. I was just going to see the Chief and explain to him why."

Leroux's phone vibrated with a message from the Chief.

Come see me immediately. Alone.

Leroux held up the phone. "Chief wants to see me alone."

Epps' phone vibrated and he laughed. "It's from the Chief. He says the op's now back with your team. We're to stand down."

"Sorry about that."

Epps waved his hands. "Hell, no need to apologize. I didn't want this op in the first place. I'm just glad I didn't kill him."

"You and me both," said Leroux as he headed for the door. "Inform my team that they're back in control and that I'm going to see the Chief."

"Will do."

Leroux stepped through the doors and past the guards. He stopped and turned to face them. "Sorry for giving you guys a hard time. If you knew what was going on, you'd understand. Thanks for not shooting."

They both laughed, the more senior responding. "Don't worry about it, sir. You were actually quite polite compared to some of the people we've had to turn away."

"So, what you're telling me is next time more junkyard dog, less pussycat?"

They chuckled. "Junkyard dog might just have got you shot."

199

Leroux grinned as he headed for the elevators. "Then status quo for next time." He climbed on the next car and sent a quick message to Sherrie.

Kane is innocent. Kill order has been aborted. More details to follow.

The reply was immediate.

Thank God. BTW, another message was sent to the Chief and one to the lone mystery number.

He replied back.

Understood.

Who the mystery number was, was now the mystery. And what had been sent? Obviously, the two messages were linked to the discovery that had just happened. So, who was the mole? Who could know that quickly? It was no one from his team, but was it someone from Epps'? He didn't think so, because they hadn't been involved until just recently, so they weren't even read in on what was occurring, though it was still possible.

He cursed as he headed toward Morrison's office. He wanted to know the truth, the entire truth, but at least he knew the most important piece of it—his friend was innocent but still up to something. The question was, what the hell was he up to? And why did no one in the CIA know what was going on, especially now that two of their operatives were involved?

Kane's off-the-books Operations Center

Outside Bethesda, Maryland

Fang sobbed uncontrollably, a mix of relief, joy, and simple stress shaking her body. And she couldn't get the smile off her face as she and Sherrie celebrated, hopping up and down in the middle of the operations center as Tommy stared from his seat, a smile on his face. Fang finally pushed away, grabbing a tissue from a Kleenex box sitting on the workstation. She blew her nose then wiped her eyes with a second tissue before sighing heavily as she dropped into one of the chairs. "And he said nothing else?"

"No, just 'More details to follow.' My guess is, whatever's going on is still actively going on. He just wanted you to know that Dylan was no longer a target."

Fang tossed her head back, exhaling loudly. "He better have a good explanation for this or I'm going to kill him myself."

Sherrie laughed and gestured at the screen. "There is that last message. Maybe it has the explanation, just in case the in-person explanation isn't good enough."

Fang chuckled. "You mean, let me read that then give me time to cool off?"

"Exactly."

"That might be one of the smarter things he's ever done." She reached up and pulled at her hair. "God, I wish he could have told me what he was up to. I've been worried sick."

Tommy cleared his throat. "He's still in North Korea. That doesn't worry you?"

Fang batted a hand. "No, he's on the job and he's good at what he does. And now that Langley knows what's going on, he's got their full support plus a Delta unit in-country with him. Right now, I'm no more worried than I ever am when he's on assignment."

Sherrie patted her on the shoulder. "So, just another day at the office then?"

Fang laughed. "I guess so."

"What do we do now?" asked Tommy.

"We stick to the job."

"Isn't the job over? I mean, we've done our part."

Fang shook her head, pointing at the display. "There are still more messages to be sent, and we still need to figure out who the two mystery callers are."

"Isn't Langley on that?"

Sherrie sat in one of the spare chairs. "Yup, but aren't you supposed to be the whiz kid when it comes to telecommunications?"

"That's what they tell me."

"Then maybe now that we know Dylan is innocent in all this, we start focusing our attention on helping him, and figuring out who the hell these other people are he's got involved, because like you said, he's still in North Korea with no way to communicate with us."

Tommy faced his station, his fingers already flying. "Then let's start breaking some laws."

Director Morrison's Office, CIA Headquarters

Langley, Virginia

Leroux rushed into the Chief's office, still in shock as to what they had just discovered—and at the moment, he had no explanation for it. How could two of the Agency's top operatives be in North Korea in an obviously coordinated op, without anyone in the Agency knowing beyond an apparent mole that had yet again shown how inside the loop they were by triggering two more messages the moment the discovery was made that Dr. Burkett was indeed Jack?

Morrison pointed at Leroux's customary chair as the door closed a little harder than usual. Leroux dropped in the chair, his mouth already in motion. "Sir, I assume you've heard that Burkett is actually Jack? The kill order has been aborted and Delta is standing down." He threw his hands up. "What the hell is going on? I mean, this is insane! There's no way the two of them defected." He paused for a split second before continuing to think aloud. "Of course there's no way. Jack was pretending to be Burkett. He was kidnapped from the office building Burkett was supposed to be working in. That's not how you do a defection. My God, what the hell is going on?"

Morrison smiled slightly. "If you shut up, I'll tell you."

Leroux's jaw dropped as his eyes shot wide. "Wait a minute, you know?"

"Yes, I know exactly what's going on, and I've been dying to tell you but I haven't been able to until now."

A mix of emotions whipped through his system, a combination of shock, relief, and anger, along with a hint of nausea that threatened to overwhelm him. He gripped the arms of his seat as he inhaled sharply. "What's going on?"

"It's actually quite the op Kane cooked up. Two months ago, one of this nation's top nuclear scientists retired. The man is a genius by all accounts, but he decided at sixty-five he would keep his promise to his wife and retire and spend more time with her, something I applaud him for, obviously."

Leroux flicked an impatient wrist. "Of course."

"A week after retiring to a retreat they had purchased in Colorado, his wife reported him missing. Because of who he was and the security clearances he had, indicators were flipped, and we became involved. It didn't take us long to determine the North Koreans had kidnapped him, obviously to work on their failed nuclear power program, and then perhaps even their weapons program. The man is as smart as Burkett is purported to be, just without the obnoxious social tendencies."

Leroux paused. "Wait a minute. Burkett, is he real?"

Morrison held up a hand. "I'm getting to that. By the time we figured out that Dr. Gorman was in North Korea, it was too late. We knew he'd be buried deep within their system, and the chances of getting to him would be next to nothing because of the nature of his work. A file was automatically flagged and released, and that's when we discovered the analysis that had been done by the real Dr. Burkett, who is every bit as brilliant and arrogant as Jack has been playing him. That analysis revealed what the Russians had been doing to subvert the North Koreans' nuclear ambitions. It was confirmed that Dr. Gorman possessed the knowledge to figure out what the planted design flaw was, and that he'd be able to correct it given enough time. Then about a month ago, his daughter and granddaughter disappeared, which could mean only two things."

Leroux leaned back. "That he was cooperating and they were being brought to him as a reward, or he wasn't cooperating and they were going to be used as leverage."

"Exactly. So, I called Kane in to discuss options, and he came up with the plan that you and everyone else have been drawn into. We planted Jack at a new job posing as Burkett, then had Kane fake his own defection, convince the North Koreans he was sincere, then give them the name of Burkett and the new job location along with the security surrounding him. The North Koreans took the bait, kidnapped him, brought him to their territory, and if all goes well, are going to deliver Jack, who if he played his part right will have also convinced them to have Kane accompany him, they're going to deliver them both into the same facility that Gorman is in."

Leroux shook his head. "Holy shit! That's insane! And when they get there, what are they going to do?"

"Well, with Bravo Team in position, they're going to kill him and die in the process, kill him and escape with the assistance of Bravo Team, or rescue him and escape with Bravo Team. And then of course, possibly die in the escape along with Bravo Team."

"So, this is a potential suicide mission."

"They both knew going in that they might not be coming out, but the risk is too high. That nation with a stable nuclear power supply is dangerous, and the nuclear waste that it produces would be worth a fortune on the black market. We could have dirty bombs going off constantly all over the planet if that reactor is allowed to fire up."

"Can't we just blow it up, or call in an air strike?"

Morrison shook his head. "No, they've had fissile material on site for a couple of decades. We could create a nuclear disaster that wipes out half of eastern China, which could lead to a nuclear war that would wipe out the rest of us."

"But wait a minute. What about the mole? Who's been triggering those messages?"

Morrison grinned. "You're looking at him."

Leroux cursed and laughed as he twisted his head away. "You're effing kidding me. You're the mole?"

Morrison shrugged. "Who better? You would never suspect me, and I have access to everything. And half the messages were going to me regardless."

"But wait a minute, a message just went to you."

"I just send the codes at the appropriate time. I didn't realize one was coming to me." He held up his phone and Leroux rose, leaning over to read it.

"So far, so good, don't forget to let everyone know the truth, especially Fang." Leroux sat back down. "So, what now?"

"Now we do everything we can to keep our eyes on him and do whatever we can to help get all three of them out of there if possible. Our people at a minimum."

Leroux finally thought to ask the question burning inside him since this began. "Why did he lie to us? Why did you guys lie to us, especially Fang?"

Morrison frowned. "That was the worst part of it, for both of us, especially for him, but it was necessary. We needed genuine reactions from everybody just in case there was indeed a mole. You know that for years now the Agency has suspected there's at least one mole within the organization. We couldn't risk them finding out what was going on and passing it on to the North Koreans. It was essential that every single one of you reacted the way you did. Betrayed, shocked, disbelief. If any of you had known the truth and acted in an unexpected way, or overacted, if that had been picked up on, Kane would be dead and perhaps even Jack." Morrison paused, regarding him. "How do you feel about that?"

Leroux shrugged. "I understand it now that it's put in context. And I'm relieved that what I suspected all along was correct." He smirked. "I'm not sure how understanding Fang is going to be."

Morrison chuckled. "Oh yeah, that was the only part of the op that he was afraid of—the ass-kicking he was going to get from Fang if he ended up surviving."

Leroux laughed. "I'd die to get that on tape so we can play it at his retirement party."

Morrison snorted. "You find out where and when it's happening, and I'll have a team put in the surveillance equipment." He pointed at the door. "Now, go bring your team up to speed and save our people's lives."

Leroux rose then paused. "But wait. The two unidentified numbers. Who are they? One of them just got a message."

"That message was to Dawson's people. Knowing Kane, he was taunting them."

"And the other, the one that's already received a message and is due to receive another at some point?"

"I have no idea. He wouldn't tell me. He said it was his backup plan."

"And when are you supposed to trigger that second message?"

"The moment the shit hits the fan."

Leroux headed for the door then froze. "Sir?"

"Yes?"

"If you knew all along, why didn't you stop Delta from executing their orders?"

Morrison pointed to a set of comms sitting on his desk. "I was jacked in the entire time and was about to give the abort order when

Atlas recognized Jack. Kane and Jack were never in any danger. At least not from us."

"Cutting it a little close?"

Morrison smiled. "It makes things more interesting, don't you think?"

Sunchon Airbase

Sunchon, North Korea

Pak shook Kane's hand. "I'll be traveling separately. I need to brief Command on the new arrangement. You two will be okay on your own?"

Kwan grinned and patted Kane's chest. "I think we'll find a way to pass the time."

Kane smiled down at her. "Now, now, be polite. I do believe you're making the major uncomfortable."

Pak said nothing, though it was clear he didn't like the sexual aspect of the relationship between his operative and his defector. Pak glanced over at another vehicle. "I'll see you at the power plant."

Kane nodded. "Looking forward to it."

Pak walked away and Kane helped Kwan into the back seat then joined her. The car immediately pulled away, escorted by leading and trailing vehicles. Kwan reached forward and closed the divider between them and the driver.

"I think that went well."

Kane had to be careful what was said here. He was still the defector, Jack was still Burkett, and they still hadn't laid eyes yet on Dr. Gorman. Plenty could still go wrong here. The fact Dawson's team hadn't killed him meant they had figured things out in time, or Morrison, monitoring the op, had called off the kill shot.

He smiled slightly. He could just imagine the expressions on their faces when Jack stared up at the eye in the sky. "Yes, I think it did go well." He forced a frown. "Though I'm not too happy I have to play BFF with that arrogant asshole."

Kwan's hand traveled up his inner thigh. "I think I can take your mind off of that for a while."

He smiled down at her as she reached her prize. "I think you and I are going to get along just fine if you keep thinking like that."

She undid his belt with her teeth and his heart raced with anticipation for what was to come as his stomach protested with the guilt over Fang. He had to remember this was an op, and they had both agreed that it wasn't cheating if it was on an op. She just didn't want to know about it. It was part of the job, and unfortunately, due to the nature of it, it was a pleasurable part of the job. It was different this time though. At least it had been last night. Because up until now, Fang had assumed he was a traitor to his country, and not only had betrayed everything and everyone he knew, but her as well.

He groaned as she reached her destination and he leaned back, spreading his arms across the seat back. He closed his eyes, enjoying the exquisite sensations while he planned out the rest of the op that so far had been going perfectly. Unfortunately, now they were heading into the unknown, the black box part of the operation that couldn't be planned for beyond contingencies. They would be going in with no weapons and no idea how much access they would be given to the kidnapped scientist. If he could get his hands on Gorman, he could snap his neck in a heartbeat, and the North Korean nuclear power program would be just as crippled as it always was.

It was unfortunate that they now knew about the design flaw in the Russian-provided plans, but Gorman would have discovered it eventually regardless. Now they would know about it and that their major source of expertise, the Russians, couldn't be trusted anymore. It should, however, still set them back at least another decade, by which time perhaps cooler heads will have prevailed on the peninsula.

The ultimate goal was to find a way to get free of security and the reactor, with Gorman in tow, meet up with Bravo Team, then get safely out of the country. The chances of that happening were slim to none, which was why he had that final message queued up for Fang. The Chief would explain to her why he had done what he had done, but she deserved one final message saying goodbye, and telling her how much he loved her and how sorry he was for causing her pain.

He just prayed he made it out of here alive so she'd never have to read it.

He had been in impossible situations before, yet they only appeared impossible to those without his skill set. And he usually had some sort of communications capability. Unless by some miracle Dawson's team could do a handoff, they would be blind the entire time, praying that

Langley and Bravo Team anticipated their next move. No matter what happened, it would be exciting, and it just might be the last exciting thing he ever did.

And if it was, it broke his heart that his last sexual encounter was with a woman like this, instead of the woman he loved.

God, what I would give to just hold you in my arms one last time.

Sunchon Airbase Perimeter

Sunchon, North Korea

Dawson and his team were now well back from the road. Kane and the others had left the airport under armed escort, so their original op was essentially over, though he suspected a new one was about to begin, one they would have to come up with on the fly.

"Zero-One, Control Actual, do you read, over?"

Fist bumps were exchanged as everyone recognized Leroux's voice. Dawson activated his comms. "Affirmative, Control. We read you. Good to have you back online, over."

"Good to be back. Has anyone brought you up to speed?"

Dawson glanced at the others. "Is *anybody* actually up to speed? I got the impression that the entire intelligence community of the United States was just caught with its pants down."

Everyone laughed including Leroux. "I know mine were around my ankles. The Chief was aware of the op, but he couldn't tell us. They needed genuine reactions from everybody."

Dawson leaned against a nearby tree. "So, can you tell us what's going on?"

"Yes, I just got a full briefing. There's a scientist named Dr. Gorman. His file has been sent to your tactical computer. He was kidnapped two months ago by the North Koreans. He's the actual nuclear genius that we're afraid will be able to get the North Korean nuclear energy program up and running very quickly. Jack was sent in as a decoy to gain access to Gorman, and in order to get him in position, Kane had to pretend to defect then dangle the fake Dr. Burkett as the carrot that could really lead to the breakthrough they needed."

"So, what's happening now? What are our orders?"

"Unfortunately, we're all flying blind on this one. The plan was to try to get Jack in as Burkett and convince the North Koreans to allow him and Kane to meet up with Gorman. At the moment, it appears they've been successful, as everyone's heading to the reactor."

"And what's the plan when they get there?"

"That all depends on what they find on the ground. We've had detailed plans of the reactor complex for years, and both Kane and Jack have familiarized themselves with everything they should encounter inside from a hardened standpoint. It's the human and added security hardware that are black boxes to us."

"I assume you've got every satellite you can get on that location?"

"We have since the moment the so-called Burkett became known to us. We've been recording everything, including all the patrol patterns and stations, twenty-four-seven. We can get you in, we can get you out, assuming you survive what's inside, but I'm not going to lie to you. This could turn into a Charlie-Foxtrot in a heartbeat."

Niner rolled his eyes. "Can't they all?"

Dawson agreed. "I'm assuming neither he nor Jack have comms?"

"No, they couldn't risk anything being found on their persons. All we can do is anticipate what they could do, and make sure we're ready for whatever ends up happening."

Dawson brought up the map on his tactical computer. "Well, that's all well and good, and we'd like to help, but we're going to have a hell of a time getting in position if this is going down any time soon. It's not like we can just take the main road."

"No, you can't, and we've been working on that. We're going to get you to head back on the road you came in on for two klicks, then there's what appears to be a utility road cut through the forest that runs straight north. That's going to take you almost the entire way, and as far as we can tell, it's not patrolled."

"Somebody has to use it," muttered Atlas. "Otherwise, it wouldn't be there."

"My friend has a point," said Dawson.

"I have no doubt he's right," replied Leroux. "But nobody's seen anything on the road in the entire time we've been monitoring, and we checked satellite footage for the past twenty-four hours and nothing's been on it. If you can get to it, you should be able to go full throttle depending on conditions."

Spock cocked an eyebrow. "Control, has anybody actually zoomed in on this thing to see if it's overgrown?"

J. ROBERT KENNEDY

"Yes, we have and it does appear a little rough, but the forest has been kept back, which could suggest it is well used and just hasn't been for the past twenty-four hours, or it could also mean that an extremely efficient communist regime has been keeping that road clear for the past sixty years and just has forgotten why."

Heads bobbed among the group, for it was a perfectly good explanation.

"An order was given in 1962 and the person who gave it is long dead, and the reason long forgotten." Dawson pushed away from the tree. "Understood, Control. We're going to retrieve our bikes and head to that road. We don't have any time to waste jawing about it. We'll contact you when we're about to get underway, over."

"Copy that, Zero-One. Control, out."

Dawson swirled a finger in the air. "Let's go, gentlemen. I hope you're all wearing athletic supports because I have a funny feeling our balls are going to get a workout on that road."

Nyongbyon Nuclear Scientific Research Center
Nyongbyon, North Korea

Kane climbed out of the car, far more relaxed than a man in his position should be—Kwan was extremely well-trained. He noticed the driver give her a look as she stepped out. It was clear none of the North Koreans were happy with the part she was playing in this, yet they had to remember she *was* just playing a part. She wasn't just there for sex. This was a full-on girlfriend experience. Her job was to make his entire life pleasurable, his new existence tolerable, and if at any time in his presence she showed anything but delight at what her current assignment entailed, it would blow the entire experience, and if he weren't also playing a part, force him to request a replacement.

Kwan caught the look, shifting uncomfortably, and Kane wrapped an arm around her protectively. He understood he meant nothing to her. She was just doing a job, a job she couldn't refuse in a country like this. He did feel sorry for her, though he couldn't show that, yet he could still be chivalrous to a point.

He glared at the driver. "Do we have a problem here?"

The man stared at him with disdain. "No."

"Good. Let's just remember the parts we're all playing here, and that we're all doing this for the good of this country, whether that's classified telephone book like me, companion like her, or glorified chauffeur like you, everybody deserves respect. Agreed?"

The man's eyes blinked rapidly for a moment before he looked away. "Yes, sir. I agree." He turned to Kwan. "I apologize."

Kwan gave a curt nod, but said nothing. The driver headed over to another vehicle, leaving them alone. Kwan held Kane tighter. "Thank you."

He ran his fingers through her hair. "For what?"

"For treating me like a person."

"You and I both know what this is, but nothing says it has to be demeaning." Now he truly felt sorry for her and his instinct to save her kicked in, but he had to shove it down and bury it hard. There was no way he could start developing feelings for this woman. No, they weren't romantic, but they were protective. Even in his days of debauchery, he always treated the women he paid for sex extremely well, compensating them far more than they were accustomed to, and treating them like gold. The sad fact was that while Kwan could indeed be a woman he might develop feelings for if Fang weren't in the picture, this entire op was likely ending in the next twelve hours, perhaps even in the next twelve minutes. And while she might be developing feelings for him, they certainly didn't run deep enough for her not to put a bullet in his head the moment she discovered the truth. She was an enemy agent and wouldn't hesitate to kill him, and he had to remember that, because he might have to kill her to accomplish his mission.

And that would truly hurt, for he hated killing anyone he made love to.

Another vehicle pulled up and Jack, still in his Burkett role, emerged. When Kane had volunteered Jack for the mission, Jack had immediately agreed, not that he had much of a choice. The man was perfect for the role and was eager to play the arrogant asshole the Burkett persona demanded. And from the little bit Kane had seen so far, he was excelling. Everyone hated him, including Dr. Ri, who emerged from the car with him, no doubt having intended to grill North Korea's newest asset, but instead subjected to an hour of well-rehearsed lectures on how Burkett was superior in every way. Kane suppressed a smile, wishing he could have listened in.

Ri stormed over to a group of officers and both Kane and Kwan listened in, though no one here beyond Jack was aware Kane spoke Korean.

"What are they saying?" he whispered, and Kwan giggled.

"He's saying that Dr. Burkett is an ignorant buffoon and as soon as they have what they need out of him, he wants to personally shoot him."

Kane chuckled. "Yeah, from what I've heard about that guy, he makes friends nowhere he goes."

She stared up at him. "Unlike you."

He winked and gave her a quick peck on the lips. "Well, some people are easy to be friends with."

A chopper thundered toward them and everyone turned to see the Soviet-built Mil Mi-2 helicopter bounce to a landing nearby, the rotors slowing as the passengers disembarked, including Major Pak. He marched toward them, his expression grim, his thin lips suggesting he wasn't pleased about something. Kane braced for whatever was about to be said, though for the moment no guns were redirected at him.

Kane took the initiative. "What's with the sourpuss?"

This caught Pak off-guard and he stared back at him, puzzled. "What?"

"It means, what has you upset?"

"A foot patrol near the airport has failed to report in. We've just sent out search parties to look for them."

Bravo Team had no doubt been in the area and might have been forced to take out a patrol. He had no problem with the patrol being dead, but now that it had been discovered, any additional troops in the area could hinder Bravo Team from repositioning to provide assistance here.

They might not be able to count on them when the pinch came.

"Could they just be late? My understanding is a lot of your men don't carry radios."

Pak eyeballed him. "How do you know that?"

Kane gave him a look. "Hello, I'm a spy. I'm supposed to know these things."

Pak relaxed slightly. "Yes, of course. Yes, it could be that they're late, maybe one of them twisted an ankle, but if that's the case, we'll find them as soon as our men trace their route. But in the meantime, we have to assume the worst."

"And what's that?"

"That your country has inserted a team to kill you and Dr. Burkett."

Kane faked concern, glancing about furtively. "Then we better get inside, shouldn't we? I'm just starting to like this place."

Pak agreed and led them inside the massive complex housing one of the most expensive failures in North Korean history that would soon be online if the mission failed. The powers that be back home were hoping that if they could eliminate or extract the expertise, in other words, deal with Dr. Gorman, that, coupled with the distrust the North Koreans would have for anything the Russians said, should set them back another decade.

And a lot can change in ten years.

As they approached the main entrance, Kane took in everything. The doors, windows, and layout were all familiar to him, and matched the plans he had memorized. What he was watching for were guard positions, gun emplacements, cameras, motion detectors, anything that would be useful when they attempted to escape. So far, everything matched up with the last briefing he had received just before his insertion, and it confirmed what he already knew.

This was next to impossible, and very well could be a suicide mission.

Everything hung on a little bit of luck, and on Bravo Team being in position when they were needed. Then one hell of an extraction plan that no one had been preparing for until the truth was revealed.

He stepped through the doors to find the place crawling with personnel, some uniformed, most in lab coats, the color-coding no doubt signifying their level of importance. There'd be no sneaking around this place if the lobby were any indication. The nature of this mission might have just been settled.

It was a suicide mission after all.

Operations Center 2, CIA Headquarters
Langley, Virginia

Leroux sat at his station, bringing himself up to speed on the new intel released to him now that the truth was out there. The flaw in the reactor design, its discovery by the real Burkett, the kidnapping of Gorman and later his family. So much had been going on that he was unaware of, that it now all made sense why Kane had done what he had done. This mission couldn't fail, it had to succeed, so everyone had to react exactly as they should.

And he felt horrible for some of the thoughts he had had about his best friend. He should have never doubted him, no matter what the seemingly insurmountable evidence showed. Kane was loyal, and Leroux could only see him betraying his country for two reasons—when his country was wrong, like with the previous North Korean incident and the kidnapped scientists, or when it came to friends or family.

The question now was how to safely extract Kane and Jack, and if possible, Dr. Gorman. There was no way any of them would be left alone. There was no slipping their tail here. They would either incapacitate or kill whoever was guarding them, then, depending on where that happened and how, escape the complex either undetected or on the run. Then, if by some miracle they made it off the grounds to wherever Bravo Team was, they would then make their escape, which at the moment was by motorcycle, of which they had only six, so three of them would have to double up, slowing their escape.

But if any of this went detected, which he couldn't see how it wouldn't, half the North Korean army would be scrambled to find them, making it nearly impossible for them to reach the coast then out to the submarine.

He growled in frustration and Tong turned toward him.

"What's up?"

He shook his head. "I'm just trying to figure out how the hell we can get them out of there before they get themselves killed."

"I have to think Kane has some sort of backup plan."

Leroux agreed. "Yes, but what? Why he wouldn't tell the Chief is beyond me. I think the key is those two messages to that unknown number. I think that's his backup plan. He triggered the preparation with the sending of the first message, and then the final one will activate the plan."

"And when is it due to be sent?"

"The moment the shit hits the fan, according to the Chief."

"So, how do we help in a plan that we have no clue what it involves?"

"Well, it can't be some big operation, can it?" asked Child, spinning in his chair as he stared at the ceiling. "I mean, if we don't know about it, then the Pentagon certainly doesn't, so it has to be something that he's arranged on the side, something private."

Tong regarded him. "What, you mean like mercenaries or something?"

Child shook his head. "No, I think it's something far more subtle. More Bond, less Rambo."

Leroux's head slowly bobbed. "Okay, let's assume you're right. How do we help?"

Child shrugged. "I don't know, I just work here."

Leroux smirked. "Not for long, with that attitude."

"Burned!" yelled Therrien from the back of the room.

Child's spin was accompanied by a raised bird. He dropped his foot, coming to a halt. "Okay, fine. If I'm trying to escape the North Korean army in their own country, how do I do it?"

Leroux folded his arms and stared at the young man. "You tell me."

"Okay, the current plan, as we think it is, is for him to escape with the assistance of Delta. Then they go over land on those bikes to the sea. They swim out or meet a Zodiac or something that'll take them to the sub. Then they leave. That's my understanding, right?"

"Yes."

"And do we think that can actually succeed?"

"Hell, no!" said Therrien. "The North Koreans are going to know they're heading for the coast, so they're going to put everything they can there. There's no way in hell that plan is going to work. All it does is prolong their deaths."

"Exactly," said Child. "So, how do you make the plan work?"

Tong leaned forward. "I don't know. How?"

Child shrugged. "I don't know, you guys are the ones with all the experience. All I'm telling you is that Kane is counting on you guys figuring it out, because if he's got a contingency set up, it's an alternative to the plan we think is the plan. And if we don't figure that out, even his contingency is going to fail. Really, what are the other options? They can hide out in North Korea until things settle down, which obviously isn't going to happen, or they can make it north to the Chinese border, but it has the same problems as reaching the coastline. The North Koreans will just blanket it. So, what is his plan that circumvents that?"

Leroux smiled slightly. "How do you get through a cordon of personnel waiting for you?"

Tong leaned even more forward. "Well, you can't penetrate it with force, because then you reveal your position, and you'll never be able to make it to your sub or whatever you have planned."

"Agreed." Leroux smiled. "And that's the answer."

Tong's eyes narrowed. "What do you mean?"

"What happens when you have a whole cordon set up to catch somebody, and then that person attempts to break the line?"

"The entire line converges on the one location."

"Exactly. So, how do we get our people through that line without triggering it?"

Her jaw dropped. "You make them think it's being penetrated somewhere else."

Leroux snapped his fingers at her. "Exactly! If we create some sort of diversion that redirects their entire response, that could leave them free and clear to escape."

Tong sat upright. "So, we need a diversion big enough to attract the entire North Korean response, but not so big that it triggers a war."

Leroux rose, heading for the doors. "Everybody start brainstorming ideas. I'm going to talk to the Chief and see just what options are available to us that the president isn't going to veto." He pushed through the doors and headed for the elevator, his mind puzzling out just what Kane had planned that didn't involve any military or intelligence assets.

And he continued to come up blank.

En route to Nyongbyon, North Korea

Dawson was nearly at full throttle as they raced down this surprisingly well-maintained service road. On their way, they had passed what appeared to be two abandoned installations, which suggested the theory this road was maintained for reasons long forgotten was correct. And if that were the case, the chances of them coming across anybody were greatly reduced. His comms squawked in his ear.

"Zero-One, Control, come in, over."

He activated his mic. "Control, Zero-One. Go ahead, over."

"Zero-One, we've got a massive increase in activity in your area. It looks like they've noticed their patrol is missing."

Dawson cursed. The news wasn't unexpected, and in fact, he was amazed they had gotten away with it for so long. "Copy that, Control. Any evidence they've located us?"

"Negative. It looks like they're deploying search teams now to your south, probably their original patrol route. But they're also deploying around the nuclear plant."

Dawson cursed again. It meant somebody had made the logic leap from two guys out on patrol who hadn't yet reported in, to possible connection with their defector and the nuclear physicist they had just abducted. It meant they would be blanketing the area, especially once they found the bodies. "Control, anything on the road ahead?"

"Negative, Zero-One. The road is still clear, though for how long, we don't know. And they've just started to deploy air assets."

Dawson glanced up. The canopy overhead was pretty thick, which should provide them with adequate cover, especially if they had enough warning to get off the road. "Copy that, Control. Keep us posted on anyone approaching the roadway so that we have time to take cover."

"Stand by, Zero-One."

Dawson raised a hand as he eased off the throttle, everyone behind him slowing.

"Zero-One, take cover! We have a chopper inbound to your position, over."

Dawson cursed as he slammed on his brakes. "Copy that, Control, taking cover."

With the sounds gone of the bike jostling on the road, the whine of the electric engine, and the wind out of his ears, he could hear the thumping of the chopper as it approached. He twisted the throttle, guiding himself into the thick of the trees as the others did the same behind him. He shut off the engine, killing any lights or electronics that might be detected should the North Koreans have sophisticated enough scanners, which he doubted.

He peered up at the chopper overhead. He could see the shadow it cast as it passed by, but nothing else, which should mean the same for its crew when it came to him and his men. The clap of the rotors slowly faded, and Dawson breathed a little easier. "Control, Zero-One, report."

"It doesn't look like they're paying any attention to you, but they have adjusted their course. They're now following the road you were on and they've slowed down. I get the distinct impression they weren't aware it was there."

"Copy that, Control. We're going mobile again. Keep us posted on any changes. Zero-One, out." Dawson started his motorcycle then returned to the road. Niner came up beside him then swatted his shoulder to get his attention. "What?"

Niner jerked a thumb behind them. "Do you think they're going to notice those?"

Dawson glanced over his shoulder. "What?"

"Our tire tracks."

Dawson cursed at the half-dozen distinct impressions they were leaving behind them, his team likely the only people that had traveled this road in a dog's age. "Nothing we can do about that now except put as much distance between us and those bodies as we can, as fast as we can." He signaled the team to proceed and took point as he rapidly gained speed. They still had approximately twenty miles to go, which shouldn't take them too long if they didn't encounter any hostiles. His concern now was the fact they had left a trail of breadcrumbs straight to themselves, and for the moment, he couldn't see any solution to the problem except a lucky rain, and from the blue skies overhead, that wasn't in the forecast. All they could hope for was that the fading light of evening would disguise their route from the naked eye, though he had a feeling the North Korean pilot would have already called in for someone to start checking the road.

Though perhaps that was premature.

"Control, Zero-One. Any evidence they found the bodies yet?"

"Negative, Zero-One," replied one of Leroux's team. "But they are closing in on the site. If they're thorough, I suspect a maximum of thirty minutes before they discover what's actually going on."

"Understood, Control. And when does the sun begin to set?"

"Approximately ninety minutes. But in those trees, you should notice the effect much sooner. We recommend night vision, no lights, when it becomes necessary."

Dawson glanced back at the others with a smile. "Thanks for the advice, Control."

The woman at the other end laughed. "Sorry, Bravo Team. Just doing my job."

"And we appreciate it, Control. There is at least one baby on this trip." He glanced over at Niner who gave him the finger.

"Funny how he knew you were talking about him," said Atlas.

"Cut the chatter, gentlemen," said Dawson. "Focus on the road. We're racing the sun now, because once we're on night vision, we're going to have to slow down a hell of a lot, which means any extraction attempt tonight could be brutal."

Kane's off-the-books Operations Center

Outside Bethesda, Maryland

"I've got something!" exclaimed Tommy.

Fang spun toward him, her nervous energy having her pacing a hole in the floor. "What is it?" she asked as Sherrie turned in her chair to face the young man.

"Our mystery number. I found other activity on it."

"Where?"

"It's been called from *this* facility on several occasions, but it's a relay to disguise the number."

"Can you figure out what number it's calling?"

"Yes, the relay is actually in the system here."

Sherrie's eyes narrowed. "What do you mean?"

"I mean the system is dialing the number we see, that number is actually being picked up here in this room, and then being relayed to its final destination."

"Why the hell would it do that?"

Tommy shrugged. "To make anybody who saw the original number think it's local?"

"Well, where is it actually going?"

"China."

Fang tensed as she took an involuntary step back. Whenever her former homeland was involved with anything, it made her nervous, especially with what had happened to her what felt like only months ago. But there was no way Kane would involve the Chinese government in what he was doing. "Do we know who belongs to that number?"

Tommy shook his head. "No. I could call it, or at least ping it and see where it is."

Sherrie looked up at Fang. "What do you think? If this number is his backup plan, knowing where that phone is might give us some indication as to what his extraction plan is."

Fang chewed her cheek for a moment. The smart move would be to leave it alone, but things had changed. The idea had been floated earlier by them and by Langley to call the numbers to see who was at the other end, but the concern raised at the time, entirely valid, was that it could tip off the traitor Kane that they were on to him. But now that they knew he wasn't a traitor and he was still on their side, that was no longer a concern. "Ping it."

Sherrie firmly agreed. "She's right. Ping it."

Tommy shrugged. "Hey, I only work here. What do I know?" He tapped at the keyboard then faced the rear wall. Fang turned to see a map showing the Korean peninsula with a flashing red dot.

"What the hell?"

Nyongbyon Nuclear Scientific Research Center
Nyongbyon, North Korea

Jack—just Jack—was having a ball playing the role of Dr. Burkett. When Kane had approached him about the mission, he didn't hesitate to join despite the distinctively one-way nature of it. It was too important. Every mission he went on, he expected he could die, though he obviously didn't hope for it. But if he was going to die, then this was the type of mission he'd want to be remembered giving his life for. Setting North Korea's nuclear power ambitions back another decade was well worth it and could save countless lives. As long as this insane regime was forced to live in near third-world conditions, they posed a minimal threat. Give them plentiful stable power, and it could allow them to progress far quicker.

According to their handlers, they were about to meet Dr. Gorman, the man Washington was having a conniption fit over the North Koreans having snatched. The man was an expert in all things nuclear, and if he cooperated for the sake of his now kidnapped family, not only could the nuclear power program finally bear fruit, he could advance their nuclear weapons program dramatically.

The question now was, what were they going to do? The suicide mission would be to shake the man's hand, yank him in, break his neck, then either be shot immediately or face potentially years of torture before finally being killed. That obviously wasn't the preferred plan, but it was the one that would at least guarantee the success of the primary mission.

Bravo Team was supposed to be in-country, but that didn't necessarily mean in position. He had landed at an airport outside of Pyongyang, which is where Bravo Team was to have eliminated them. They were now sixty miles north of that, and while his journey on paved roads breezing through checkpoints took less than an hour and a half, he had to imagine that Bravo Team would take longer, and with no comms, there was no way they could know they were in position to help.

The next question was, should they attempt to delay as long as possible before making their move, or just make it the first time the opportunity presented itself and attempt their escape, hoping Bravo Team was in place. Kane had said he had a contingency plan should they make it off the grounds with transportation, but without Bravo Team, he couldn't see them possibly escaping based upon the number of guards he had seen outside.

Dr. Ri pointed to the elevators. "Are you ready to meet Dr. Gorman?"

Jack nodded, adjusting his bright yellow lab coat he and Kane had been given moments ago. "Absolutely, it's always a pleasure to meet one of the old guard who was wise enough to step aside and make room for new ideas."

Ri bristled and Jack suppressed a smile. It was fun playing an incredibly arrogant asshole. Ri boarded the elevator first and Jack followed, receding into a corner just as his character should, and noticed with amusement that Kane's new squeeze had a fist full of his partner's ass. She was either playing the part extremely well, or Kane's legendary bedroom prowess had turned her to his side.

No one had any idea how good the files the North Koreans had on Kane were. It was long suspected there was a mole within the CIA feeding intelligence to the Chinese, and with the Chinese and North Koreans' allies, there was a distinct possibility the information on assets that operated in the area could have been shared. If the North Koreans were aware Kane had a girlfriend back home that he had been living with for some time, it had been decided he would request female companionship to make his defection appear more legitimate. Jack wasn't one for relationships, but judging by what he had seen of Kwan so far, he wished he was playing defector and Kane the scientist.

I always get the shit end of the assignment.

They rode up in silence, the doors opening on the third floor. Everyone filed out then Ri led the way down the long corridor, pushing one side of a double set of doors out of the way. They entered a room filled with modern computers as well as chalkboards and whiteboards filled with equations.

There were about a dozen people working but only one of them had a bright yellow lab coat like he did, and it was Dr. Gorman. Evidently, this particular color identified them as either American or non-North Korean, or perhaps it was as simple as people who couldn't be trusted therefore shouldn't be alone. It could be a problem, or it could work to their advantage, depending on how things played out.

Ri led them to the back of the room where Gorman was staring at a large screen displaying schematics of what Jack assumed were the inner workings of the nuclear reactor. "Dr. Gorman, I'd like you to meet some people."

Gorman flinched then turned, the man clearly a bundle of nerves. "If you people expect me to solve your problem, these constant interruptions aren't helping." He noticed that two white men were standing there, both wearing bright yellow lab coats, and his eyes widened as he rose. "Don't tell me they got you, too."

Jack shrugged. "Obviously they did, or at least *I* wouldn't be here."

"And you are?"

"Dr. Leonard Burkett."

Gorman regarded him. "Burkett, I know that name. I think I've read a few of your papers."

"I should hope so. Did you understand them?"

Gorman glared at him. "What the hell kind of question is that? Of course I understood them. I've been working in this field since before you were born."

"That's the problem, isn't it? Old mind, old ways of thinking, old ideas." Jack waved a hand at the monitor showing the schematics. "You still haven't figured it out, have you?"

"What are you talking about?"

"The flaw, the intentional design flaw that the Russians inserted in the design so that it would never be successful."

Gorman's jaw dropped. "I was suspecting it was something like that. I couldn't believe it was a construction error. You figured it out?"

"Long ago. That's why they've brought me in, apparently."

Gorman turned to Major Pak. "Does that mean you no longer need me, that I'm free to go, that my family are free to go?"

Pak shook his head. "I'm afraid not just yet, Doctor. Once the reactor is up and running, and we're confident the flaw has been corrected, then we'll discuss your future and the future of your family."

Gorman collapsed back in his chair, his shoulders sagging. "What did I ever do to deserve this?"

"You are one of the best in the field," replied Pak.

Jack shoved good taste aside as his character would. "I *am* the best, so why they chose me is obvious." He turned to Pak. "He's right, we don't need him anymore. He's dead weight. Let him and his family go, and let me at this. I'll have you up and running before the year is out. He'll just be in the way."

Pak regarded him. "Some might think you were trying to save Dr. Gorman from an undesirable future, though in the little bit of time I've spent with you, I don't think you care about this man at all, and all we're hearing is your supreme arrogance."

Jack shrugged. "My motivations are irrelevant, as I have no doubt anything I say will have no effect. But like I have said before, and what is extremely relevant, is that I work alone. You want me to fix your reactor, I'll fix your reactor, but keep him out of my way. In fact"—he waved the finger at the entire room—"keep them all out of the way. They will just slow me down and piss me off. Genius needs space, which means I need a whole lot of space."

"You're not the Burkett I've heard about," said Gorman glaring up at him.

Jack tensed. Everything he had been told indicated the real Burkett and Gorman had never met.

Pak picked up on it. "You know this man?"

Gorman shook his head and Jack relaxed slightly. "No, I've never met him. Like I said, I've read some of his papers, and I know a couple of people that have worked with him in the past. I heard he was cocky, but I never heard he was so mean."

Jack had to think quick on his feet. He laughed. "Perhaps I have become more jaded over the years. It comes from being surrounded by incompetence."

Gorman folded his arms and frowned at Pak. "He doesn't want to work with me, I don't want to work with him. Pricks like that aren't worth it."

Pak was about to say something, no doubt threatening, when Jack laughed again. "Now, there's the spirit that I expect from a genius. I'll work with him, at least for the moment. He's familiar with your setup, so he can brief me." He flicked his lab coat. "And can we do something about these? I absolutely detest bright yellow. It agitates me. Reminds me of when I was a kid and my mother forced me to wear a yellow raincoat to school, every friggin' day it rained. I got beat up enough for being infinitely smarter than everyone else at school including the teachers, but put me in one of those damned yellow monstrosities with those stupid big black rubber boots, and it made things exponentially worse. I will not work in this friggin' color." He stripped the coat off and tossed it onto the back of one of the chairs. One of the two armed guards in the room surged forward but came to a halt as Pak raised a hand.

"How about this as a compromise? While in this room, you don't need to wear it, but the moment you pass through those doors"—he pointed at the double doors at the far end of the room—"you must wear it or risk being shot."

Jack bowed his head slightly. "A reasonable compromise, though I doubt you'll risk shooting me, as I'm your only hope of a stable power supply."

Kane cleared his throat. "I'd be careful, buddy. This country has a habit of cutting off its own nose to spite its face. You might be their last best hope for stable power, but they won't hesitate to kill you if you embarrass them. They'd rather suffer for another decade than lose face."

Jack frowned at Kane. "Fine. The coat goes on the moment I walk through those doors." He turned to Gorman. "How about we get that tour going? I want to see everything. Spare no details." He glanced at

Pak. "It's probably going to take a couple of hours, if not more. If you and your people want to go elsewhere rather than being bored—"

Kane cut Pak off. "If you don't mind, Major, I think that it would be fascinating, even if I don't understand the technical details. Despite the life I've led, I've never actually been inside a nuclear power facility."

Pak glanced at Kane. "Not to worry, Mr. Kane, I'm not letting either of you out of my sight, which means where he goes you go."

Kane laughed, wrapping his arms around Kwan. "Then everything is working out just perfectly. How about when the tour is over, we all go for dinner and get to know each other a little better."

Pak frowned. "I doubt that's a good idea."

Jack raised a finger. "Well, dinner might be out of the question, but I assume we have quarters?"

"Of course. There's an entire residential section."

"Good. Then I suggest when this is over, Dr. Gorman and I go to his quarters."

Gorman stared at him. "Why would you want to go to my quarters? I can guarantee you, there's nothing special about them, and I never entertain."

Jack smiled. "I want to see yours so that I know for sure that whatever they give me is better." He jabbed a finger at Kane. "And I want him to see them as well, so he knows what he's done to me for the rest of my life."

Kane shrugged. "I'd love to see them. I have no doubt your new employers intend to take good care of you, just like they're taking good care of me." He gave Kwan a squeeze.

Jack pointed at her. "And I'm still waiting on one of those."

En route to Nyongbyon, North Korea

The North Koreans had found the bodies fifteen minutes ago, but it changed little when it came to the reality of their situation. Dawson kept them moving forward as fast as possible, and they were nearing their destination. According to Langley, more air and ground assets were rushing into the area, though most of the activity was still to the south near the airport, but was slowly expanding outward from where the bodies had been discovered. What had him more concerned was a patrol had been sent up the service road they were on. If his team kept going, there was no chance of the patrol catching them, but they were about to stop and go off the road and through the forest toward the power plant complex. The only way this still worked was if things happened quickly and, unfortunately, the timing wasn't under their control. Once they reached their destination, all they could do was wait.

He checked his GPS. They were less than a mile from where they would be turning off. They could keep going for a few more miles then double back in an attempt to confuse the enemy, but that could waste valuable time. This was the frustrating part of the mission. Without comms at Kane's end, they had no way of knowing whether he was triggering his side of the plan in five minutes, five hours, or five days. He was hoping for five minutes, which meant there weren't any to waste now attempting to trick the enemy.

He raised a hand and they slowed. He turned into the trees, praying that by the time the patrol reached this location, they might just miss the fact the tracks they had been following were no longer there.

He grunted.

Yeah, like we're going to get that lucky.

International Waters

Off the Coast of North Korea

Chan Chao leaned over the side of the decrepit fishing vessel and hurled. He could count on one hand how many times he'd been on a boat in his life, but he didn't have enough fingers and toes to count how many times he had thrown up on one. He and the water didn't mix, never had, never would, and he resented Kane for putting him through this. When the CIA operative had briefed him on the mission, he had called the man a fool and his opinion hadn't changed. It was a suicide mission. And by dragging him into it, Kane was just adding to the number of innocent deaths. But if the mission succeeded, it could prevent North Korea from having nuclear power, which had to be a good thing.

He was getting old, too old for this business, but he knew no different. He'd been doing it for decades. He didn't support the Chinese government, and this was his way of getting back at them for everything they had done to his beloved country. But if he and his wife were caught, they would certainly be shot, though not before brutal torture. He'd rather die out here at sea from North Korean bullets, though it broke his heart to think of his beloved wife going on alone. It would kill her. But she was a tough woman, and Kane had always promised she'd be taken care of should something happen.

He paused.

If I die tonight, Kane is most likely dying with me. That bastard.

He dismissed the thought. Kane was the type who would make provisions for such things. He would have to trust that Kane had somebody on the outside, who would see to the promises he had made even after death. But no one was dead yet, at least he assumed no one was, and for the moment, there was no reason he should be killed. He was a Chinese fisherman in Chinese waters with a legitimate fishing license. Well, perhaps legitimate was pushing the boundaries of the definition.

The satellite phone rang and his eyes narrowed as he grabbed it, hanging onto the deck railing. Only Kane had this number, and his wife, but she would never call unless there was an emergency.

He answered. "Hello?"

A woman's voice replied, speaking perfect Mandarin. "Hello? Who am I speaking to?"

He gave the phone a look. "You called me."

"Yes, I did. I'm hesitant to say my name, but I believe we have a mutual friend."

Chan was tempted to hang up, though no one should have this number but Kane, so it had to be important. The woman at the other end of the line spoke perfect Mandarin with a local dialect, and it led to a thought. "Give me your first name." There was a hesitation. "Listen, I think I know who you are."

"Who do you think I am?"

"I think you're the girlfriend of the biggest pain in my ass I've known my entire life."

She laughed. "That definitely sounds like him. Fang."

He smiled. "I'm not going to say my name because I can't be entirely certain you are who you say you are, but the fact you're calling this line tells me something's wrong."

"Not necessarily wrong." There was a sigh, triggering a burst of static. "Listen, up until a few minutes ago, we assumed our mutual friend was a traitor to his country. Now we know better. We know he sent a message to you and that another message is due to be sent shortly."

Chan picked up on that. "Shortly?"

"Well, I'm assuming shortly. According to the person who would be triggering that message to you, it was due to be sent the moment his escape attempt began."

Chan relaxed slightly. "So, you have no information on when that might be starting?"

"No. My understanding is he's in position and it could begin at any moment, or it could be days. We just don't know. We have no comms with him."

"Yes, well, I'm in position and should be able to get to the rendezvous point no matter when he starts, as long as I haven't vomited myself to death. I still don't see why you've risked calling me. Despite this call being encrypted, there is a chance someone could intercept it."

"We need to know what his plan is."

Chan tensed. "Why?"

"My last briefing tells me the North Koreans are pouring more assets into the area. We're concerned they'll create a cordon that he won't be able to get through."

"I'm sure he's got a plan for that."

"Yes, we believe he does, and that that plan involves us coordinating with you."

"Oh? Care to explain that to me?"

"The moment the truth was discovered, his contact fully briefed us. The only missing element was you. I've made contact with you against CIA orders, because I think he wanted us to talk. If we know where you are picking him up, we can have a diversion created that should draw the North Koreans away from your planned rendezvous. But if we don't know where to create that diversion, he probably has no hope in hell of getting through."

Chan pursed his lips as his stomach fought him. His wife had told him to get the Gravol suppositories and not the pills, but there was no way he was shoving something up his ass. It was the wrong choice. He sighed. "The rendezvous point is at Changp'o, one kilometer offshore."

"Aren't you concerned about patrols?"

"Of course I'm concerned about patrols. This isn't my first rodeo, as he might say. Create your diversion south of the rendezvous and that should create an opening for him to get through. And don't call this number again. I can't risk the signal being detected. As soon as I get the trigger message, I'll be tossing it overboard."

"Understood. Good luck."

"Good luck to us all." He hesitated. "One thing, Fang."

"What's that?"

"If I don't survive this, tell my wife that I'll miss her nagging."

Fang chuckled. "Are you sure you want those as your final words?"

"Oh, I'm sure my final words will be far more colorful than that, but my final words to her, yes, she'll know what they mean."

Fang's response was subdued. "I'll make sure she gets the message. And when you see Dylan, just in case you don't make it, tell him that I love him and that I forgive him."

"I will. Now goodbye. I have work to do." He ended the call then rushed to the rail, emptying his guts yet again. If he did see Kane again, he was punching him in the throat before he delivered any message from the man's girlfriend.

Nyongbyon Nuclear Scientific Research Center Perimeter

Nyongbyon, North Korea

The Nyongbyon complex was huge, almost ten square miles of land divided into two sections, one housing the reactor and all the research facilities, the other, the residential component where those that worked here lived along with their families. It reminded Dawson a little bit of military housing, though unlike back home where you were free to come and go as you pleased, this housing was surrounded by chain-link fencing rimmed with barbed wire and patrolled by armed guards.

He had familiarized himself with the area and the general layout of the major buildings. The problem was there were only six of them and there was no way they could cover the entire area. It was simply too big. Assumptions had to be made as to what Kane's plan was. He could sneak out any number of exits, but all those exits would be guarded, and he would be closely watched everywhere he went. Sneaking out was an unlikely option, so that left two other options. One was escaping in a blaze of glory, counting on them to take out any hostiles on the outside as he sprinted toward them, or alternatively, a momentary lapse by his guards taken advantage of that might buy him a few seconds, perhaps even a couple of minutes to make a partial escape that would eventually be discovered.

The question was, where did Kane think Bravo Team would be waiting? Directly in front of them was the reactor Kane and the others had entered hours before. To the right, the complex continued, to the left was the residential area. If Kane expected help, he had to know it was coming from the front—there was no way the team could provide support from any of the other directions. There were simply too many buildings in the way and too many opportunities to be discovered, with fewer opportunities to make a clean escape.

"What do you think?" asked Niner, lying prone on the ground beside him.

"I think he has to be coming out that front entrance, either in disguise or on the run."

"Maybe we should try to put a two-man team at the rear, just in case," suggested Atlas.

Dawson shook his head. "No, then we would be rescuing them after the shit hit the fan. Let's just spread along this tree line. No spotters just shooters. Once I give the order, start taking down anything in a uniform that moves."

"It would be nice to have some secondary explosions," said Spock.

"It would definitely provide a distraction," agreed Dawson. "Atlas, pick a good position that gives you a full range and choose six targets for that eighty-four. We only get one chance at it, so make them juicy."

Atlas grinned. "As juicy as Vanessa's roast chicken?"

Niner groaned. "Why did you have to mention her roast chicken? It's like incredible."

Jagger smacked his massive lips. "I've never tasted better. I can't get Costco rotisserie chicken anymore. It just doesn't taste like chicken now that I've had hers."

"Yeah, Vanessa's legs and thighs and breasts are the best." Niner squinted. "What's the chicken's ass called?"

Atlas clenched a fist. "I don't know, but if you say my girlfriend's ass is juicy, you're going to be tasting my knuckles before you taste her chicken again."

Niner shrugged. "I thought I was talking about her chicken, though her legs and thighs—"

Atlas reached across Dawson and belted Niner in the shoulder.

"Geez, a little touchy aren't we? Maybe she shouldn't be wearing sweatpants that say 'Juicy' on the ass if she doesn't want us making fun of you."

Spock cocked an eyebrow. "Us? Don't get me involved in this."

Dawson put an end to it. "Before this turns into a friendly fire incident, let's spread out. Find good cover that gives each of you full coverage of the entire area. And Atlas, watch where you're shooting that thing. Try not to hit the main building. For all we know, they keep

256

plutonium in desk drawers. Last thing we want is to trigger some sort of nuclear disaster. There'll be no end to the paperwork."

"Copy that, BD. No Chernobyls."

Niner reached over and grabbed Atlas' ass. "Now go get that juicy thing in position, sweet cheeks."

Atlas rolled away, breaking the grip on his ass as he growled. "I'm so kicking your ass when this is over."

"Promises, promises," muttered Niner as he scampered to the left, the team spreading out, preparing for what could be the biggest Charlie-Foxtrot of their careers.

Nyongbyon Nuclear Scientific Research Center

Nyongbyon, North Korea

Kane inhaled deeply as he steadied his hammering heart. This was the best damn tour he had ever been on. About an hour into the tedious boredom, where Gorman explained everything in detail to the fake Burkett, while Jack wisely said little that might risk revealing the fact he knew almost nothing about the subject at hand, Kwan had dragged him into a supply room and locked the door. Pak had said nothing, evidently quite willing to let Kwan monitor him in this controlled environment.

She had monitored part of him for the past forty minutes and he wasn't sure how to feel. The sexual component was of course fantastic, and to maintain his cover, he simply shut down the emotions that caused him guilt. But there was something else in the back of his mind now troubling him. Was his assigned companion actually falling for him? If she wasn't, she was incredibly talented at her job and deserved an Oscar for her performance. If it was all an act, then he would feel no guilt when he betrayed her. But if the poor girl was developing feelings for him, it was yet another distasteful aspect of this mission.

But this woman was supposed to be a pro. Countless women over the years who hadn't received the training she should have, had fallen for him within hours, just as she appeared to have. But he had to think she was simply putting on a spectacular show, and that when push came to shove, she wouldn't hesitate to put a bullet in his head.

And he had to remember that, because if he hesitated, it could cost lives, including his own.

"Shall we rejoin the tour?" she asked.

He smiled. "Probably a good idea. Somebody is going to ask where we are, and I'd hate for the major to get in trouble."

She giggled. "He does seem rather uptight, doesn't he?"

"Yes, he does, but I won't hold that against him. We've only ever seen him at work. I bet on a Friday night with his friends, he's a wild man."

She roared with laughter then slapped a hand over her mouth at how loud it was in their confined space.

He gave her a hug. "Let's get out of here."

She opened the door and they emerged from the supply room. Nobody paid them any mind, likely due to the color of her lab coat, a bright red, which from the people he had seen wearing the same color suggested security. He hadn't seen too many of them, nor were there many armed guards on this floor. It appeared that most security was concentrated outside of the building and in the main lobby.

They evidently trusted their staff. To a point.

It opened up some possibilities for success on this floor, but he wasn't so sure about the main floor or outside. Subterfuge could get them part of the way, and it had been long enough for Bravo Team to be in place to assist in the escape. The moment that began, Morrison would trigger the final message, Tommy would send it, Chan would receive it then move into place, then they would have one hour to escape, be captured, or killed.

Kane made eye contact with Jack at the far end of the room where Gorman was disassembling a scale model of the reactor. Jack continued to feign interest while remaining careful with anything he said. The last thing they needed was Gorman discovering he was a fraud.

A gong sounded. Kane instinctively checked his watch and frowned, the CIA-customized device he normally wore confiscated at the start of his initial interrogation. The entire room became a buzz of activity, some smiles appearing for the first time since they had arrived.

"What's going on?" he asked.

"End of the shift," said Ri as he rose from his desk nearby. "Now, I understand Dr. Burkett has ingratiated himself on Dr. Gorman, however, I suggest we all have dinner at my residence after our new arrival gets a tour of his apparent rival's quarters. My wife is expecting us and is accustomed to entertaining. I promise you a delicious meal and good conversation."

Kane smiled broadly and bowed. "We would be honored, I'm sure." He turned to Pak. "With your permission, of course."

Pak gave a curt nod. "I would never deny you the pleasure of Dr. Ri's company, especially after his wife has no doubt gone to so much trouble."

Ri smiled. "Then it's settled."

The staff in white coats filed out of the room, and an agitated Gorman, accompanied by Jack sporting a smirk, joined them. Kane turned to Jack. "So, Dr. Burkett, how was your tour?"

Jack eyed Kwan. "Not as good as yours, I think."

Kane wrapped an arm around her. "No, I doubt it was. But was it informative?"

"It confirmed what I suspected. They're decades behind, but I have no doubt I can get them operational quite quickly."

"Well, you'll be happy to hear that Dr. Ri has invited us to his home to enjoy his wife's cooking."

Jack frowned. "I'm not a big fan of Asian cuisine. No offense, but while your wife might be an excellent cook, I doubt I could stomach it."

Ri bristled and Kane held out a hand. "Have you ever eaten Korean food before?"

Jack shook his head. "Nope."

"Then you don't know what you're missing. Trust me. And besides, you better get used to it. It's not like they're going to fly McDonald's in every day to satisfy our ridiculous American palates."

Jack frowned. "You mean they don't have McDonald's here?"

Everybody stared at him. "Of course they don't have McDonald's here."

Jack shrugged, his hands palm up. "What's everybody looking at me for? I don't pay attention to garbage like that. I just know I like McDonald's." He sighed. "Fine. Let's go to Dr. Ri's and let his wife introduce me to North Korean cuisine. I'll visit Dr. Gorman's residence tomorrow."

Ri gave a curt nod then headed for the doors. "I'll go on ahead and alert my wife as to what to expect." He pushed through the double doors, the two guards on either side snapping to attention briefly. Kane had no doubt the man was delivering a warning about Jack.

The room was nearly empty now and Kane looked about. "When does your night shift arrive?"

"They don't," replied Gorman. "We only have the one shift from eight AM to six PM, six days a week. All the expertise is concentrated and working together at all times."

Kane nodded. "Efficient."

Gorman shrugged. "They seem to think so."

Pak regarded him. "You disagree?"

Gorman dismissed his own criticism with a wave of his hand. "Forget I said anything. I'm just accustomed to working in functioning reactors where everything goes twenty-four-seven. In time, this place will be the same, I'm sure, with Dr. Burkett's help."

Jack headed for the doors. "Let's go, I'm starving."

Pak cleared his throat. "Aren't you forgetting something, Doctor?"

Jack stopped and turned. "What?"

Pak pointed at the bright yellow lab coat lying on the back of a chair.

"Oh shit, yeah, I forgot about that monstrosity. We definitely have to have a talk about a change of color coding around here. I personally like those red ones your guards are wearing." He retrieved his lab coat and shrugged it on as he headed for the doors. "By the way, where's the bathroom around here? I have to drain the lizard."

Kane grabbed the guard nearest him, hauling him in and breaking his neck as Jack, who had just given the signal to act, lunged forward with a pencil and plunged it into the other guard's jugular. Gorman collapsed backward into one of the lab tables, gasping in shock as Pak reached for his weapon. Kane grabbed Kwan and put her in a sleeper hold as Jack disarmed the major, breaking his wrist in the process. Pak collapsed to his knees, wincing in agony, and Jack pistol-whipped him unconscious.

"Take me with you," gasped Kwan as Jack stripped out of his clothes and donned the major's uniform.

"Don't trust her," said Jack as he pulled on pants far too short for him.

"Please, Dylan, take me with you."

She was almost out cold and he quickly debated what to do. He had no intention of killing her, it wasn't necessary, though death might be the preferable choice if he didn't take her with him. If they didn't succeed in escaping, then any decision he made was irrelevant. But if he did and left her behind, she would be blamed, likely tortured for God knows how long, and as a woman, that torture would include repeated rape.

He did care for her as a person and he realized she was doing a job. The question was, was she still doing that job? If he took her with them, could he trust her, or would she betray them? He eased up and Jack cursed as he finished putting on the ill-fitting uniform.

"You have to stop thinking with Mr. Wiggly."

"You know what they'll do to her if we leave her behind."

"Yes, I do, and I know what she'll do to us the first chance she gets."

Gorman finally recovered enough to ask questions. "What's going on here? Who are you people?"

Jack extended a hand. "Nice to meet you, Doc. You can call me Jack."

"Jack? Jack who?"

"Just Jack. And to answer your next question, no, I'm not Dr. Burkett. We're here to get you out."

"You're what, like CIA or something?"

"Or something." Kane turned Kwan around to face him. "I don't know if I can trust you, and I know I shouldn't, but you and I both know what they're going to do to you when we get out of here." He pressed a finger into her chest. "But if I for one moment think you're going to betray us, I'll kill you in a heartbeat. Understood?"

"Understood." She pointed at Jack. "There's no way in hell they're going to buy that. He looks ridiculous."

Jack threw up his hands. "I agree. I feel like I'm in Oompa Loompa land."

Kwan took over. "Get out of those and put your clothes back on. White people wear yellow coats in this building without exception, so there's no point trying to hide it. The key is confidence." She held out her hand to Jack. "Give me the gun."

Jack gave her a look. "I didn't know North Koreans had a sense of humor."

She held out her hand firmly. "Give it to me. They expect me in a red coat to be armed, especially if I'm with three yellow coats."

Jack eyed Kane. "We're dead the moment I give her that gun."

Kane shook his head. "I don't think so. Besides, she's right. There's no way we can get out of here trying to disguise ourselves as Koreans. We're as honky as they come."

Jack cursed and handed over the gun. "I hope you're right about this."

Kwan took it and stuffed it into her belt. She turned to Kane. "I trust you've got a way out of here?"

"Through the front door."

She rolled her eyes. "Out of the country, not out of the building."

"I hope so."

"That doesn't exactly inspire confidence."

He shrugged. "Hey, I'm flying blind here. All I can do is hope that the other part of the plan isn't."

"Fine." She turned to Jack as he hurriedly put on his own clothes. "We better tie him up," she said, gesturing at the unconscious major. She kneeled beside the guard whose neck Kane had snapped and relieved him of his sidearm and knife. She handed them to Kane. "Hide these on your person."

"Spare mags?"

She shook her head. "He doesn't have any. They're armed to shoot a single rogue scientist making an escape, not for a sustained fight. In the lobby and outside, they'll have more ammo on them."

"Lovely." He ejected the mag to confirm there were at least some bullets in it, and was pleased to see it was full. He tucked it in his belt as Jack finished donning his yellow coat once again.

Kwan handed him a gun and knife from the second dead soldier, then turned to them all. "Do exactly what I say, when I say. I'm your armed escort to Dr. Ri's dinner at his residence. If anyone asks where the major is, tell them he had an important phone call to make to Command, and will be joining us later, but he didn't want to be rude so he had us go on ahead. Dylan, remember, you're happy to be here. Jack, if that's what your name is, you are still Burkett and you don't care where you are. And Dr. Gorman, as far as you're concerned, nothing has changed from when you came in this morning, so get that smile off your face."

Gorman's excited grin turned into a frown for a split second before it once again became a grin. "I'm sorry, I can't help it, I'm just so excited you're here."

Kane stepped closer, tapping the man's chest. "We're here, but none of us are safe yet. You keep grinning like an idiot and you're going to get us all killed. In fact, the chances of us getting out of this alive are slim and become none if you can't get that face of yours under control."

This had the desired effect and Gorman paled slightly. "You're right, of course." A thought apparently occurred to him. "What about my daughter and my granddaughter?"

"I know where they're holding them," said Kwan. "When we get out of here, I exchange that information for my freedom. Agreed?"

Kane nodded. "Agreed."

She stared at him for a moment, placing a hand on his chest. "It was all a lie, wasn't it?"

He ran his fingers through her hair and she closed her eyes, pressing against his hand. "Not all of it."

She sighed. "Then enough of this. Let's get the hell out of here. If we hurry, we can still mix in with the others leaving the building."

Gorman led the way through the doors and down the corridor toward the elevator with Kane and Jack side-by-side, and Kwan, her weapon visible on her hip, bringing up the rear. Half a dozen people were clustered near the elevator, most with white coats, though there was one sporting yellow with a red coat providing escort. The doors chimed, and the white coats filed in, followed by the yellows, then the reds, the routine apparently well-practiced.

The other red coat turned to Kwan. "I haven't seen you here before."

Kwan growled, jerking a thumb at Kane. "I'm assigned to this one, but my major had an important phone call from Command, so now I have to babysit the three of them to Dr. Ri's house for dinner."

The guard lowered his voice. "You know what red coat means?"

"What's that?"

"Nothing but shit assignments."

Kwan laughed. "Fortunately, I'm only here for a few days."

The doors opened with a ping.

"Consider yourself lucky. I've got two more years here, at least." He stepped off then to the side and Kwan mimicked him as everyone left the elevator. The white coats headed for the exit followed by the yellows with Kwan and the other red coat again taking up the rear. Their badges were all scanned and checked against a list, and Kane was shocked at how smoothly things were going, the banter between Kwan and the other guard likely having gotten them this far without suspicion.

The woman checking the badges against a list stepped back and looked down for a moment. An alarm sounded and Kane kept character despite realizing she had activated the alarm with her foot. "What's going on?"

"Security!" shouted the woman as she ducked behind the counter. Guards rushed toward them and Kane cursed. He drew his weapon, Jack and Kwan doing the same, and Kane put a bullet in the talkative guard's chest. He relieved him of his assault rifle as Jack and Kwan opened fire, taking down half a dozen guards within moments. Kane grabbed Gorman and pushed him toward the outer doors. Gorman shoved the door aside and Jack followed as gunfire erupted outside followed by a massive explosion that shook the entire building.

And as Kane receded through the doors, opening up on the guards in the lobby with the liberated automatic weapon, he prayed there was friendly fire on the other side to join in this fight.

Nyongbyon Nuclear Scientific Research Center Perimeter

Nyongbyon, North Korea

The gunfire from inside the building was the first tip-off that shit was hitting a fan somewhere nearby. "This is it," said Dawson as he activated his comms. "Control, Zero-One. We've got activity, sounds like gunshots, over."

"Copy that Zero-One," replied Leroux, his team now in control. "You are clear to engage, repeat, you are clear to engage, over."

"Roger that, engaging now. Bravo Team, clear your arcs, Zero-Seven, hold off on that eight-four until we have eyes on target."

"Copy that, Zero-One," replied Atlas. M24 SWS Sniper Weapon Systems and M4 assault rifles opened up from the tree line. Dawson squeezed off a round from his M4, taking out one of the guards at the main gate. He acquired his next target and squeezed, the man dropping as he unslung his rifle.

Suddenly the siren inside the building was joined by a general alarm across the entire campus. The shitstorm was coming, and if Kane didn't hurry up, they were facing a Charlie-Foxtrot of epic proportions.

"Something happening at the doors," reported Niner.

"Control, Zero-One. Do you have eyes on that door?"

Leroux replied. "Stand by, Zero-One. Drone is coming into position now."

Dawson ignored the door, instead continuing to engage every target in sight as the others did the same around him. Bodies lay strewn about everywhere as civilians screamed and ducked for cover, or merely sprinted toward the residential section of the massive facility. The day shift having ended just before the action began was making things more difficult, but could do the same for the enemy with respect to Kane and the others.

"Zero-One, Control. Confirmed Dr. Gorman and Jack are coming through the doors, both wearing yellow lab coats."

"Confirmed, Zero-One," said Atlas. "I've got eyes on them through the glass."

"Then I think it's time to up the ante." Dawson glanced to his left as an engine roared, a troop carrier racing down the road toward them. "I suggest we start with that target at our nine o'clock."

"Roger that, Zero-One." Atlas leaned out from his cover, positioning the 84mm Carl Gustaf recoilless rifle on his shoulder and firing. The troop carrier erupted in a ball of flame, the soldiers in the back screaming in agony as the vehicle erupted. Dawson ignored it, instead continuing to engage the reinforcements rushing toward the area.

Kane, where the hell are you?

Operations Center 2, CIA Headquarters

Langley, Virginia

Leroux stood in the middle of the op center, his headset in place as his eyes flitted between various satellite and drone feeds as well as maps indicating North Korean activity. The doors hissed open and Morrison rushed in, joining him in the center of the room.

"Status?"

Leroux gestured at the massive display curving across the front of the room. "The shit's hitting the fan, sir. The two yellow coats you see are Dr. Gorman and Jack."

"What about Kane?"

"No sign of him yet. Wait." The main doors to the reactor complex swung open again and a yellow coat and a red coat emerged into the fading light. He snapped his fingers over his shoulder. "Facial recognition on them right now! It looks like Kane to me."

The computer grabbed a freeze-frame from the drone footage, mapping both people, confirming their identities a moment later. "It's Kane," confirmed Tong.

"And his new side-strange," said Child.

"Is she helping them?" asked Tong as the woman on the screen opened fire with an assault rifle, Kane doing the same.

"Holy shit!" exclaimed Child. "He must have one hell of a magic wand to turn her in less than twenty-four hours."

Groans and snickers rippled through the room.

"Language, Randy, we've got company," admonished Leroux before glancing at Morrison who shrugged.

"The kid's right. He must have some serious, what do you kids call it, BDE?"

Leroux snorted as an explosion flared across the screen. He turned to Tong. "Is our diversion ready?"

"Ready to go on your signal."

"Tell them to stand by." He activated his comms. "Zero-One, Control Actual. New red and yellow targets coming through the door now. Yellow is our primary, red is his North Korean companion who appears to be cooperating, over."

"Copy that, Control. Is our exfil route still clear?"

Leroux turned toward Therrien who gave a thumbs-up. "Still clear, but we've got everything in the area mobilizing. It's going to get awfully cozy there in the next fifteen minutes."

Leroux turned back toward the displays. "Affirmative, Zero-One. Exfil route is still clear, however, units from the entire region are responding. We don't expect it to be open for long."

"Copy that, Control, get ready on that diversion. We're going to need it. Zero-One, out."

Morrison lowered his voice. "I sent the message to Chan. He'll hopefully be moving into position in time."

Leroux glanced over at the map showing the coastal region and the last known location of Chan's satellite phone. The system indicated it had been shut off several minutes ago, exactly as he had promised in his conversation with Fang, a conversation he had not approved, though was pleased it had taken place. It had provided critical answers. "I think we're going to need a whole lot of luck on this one, sir."

"Luck is nothing without the skill to take advantage. If anybody can do it, it's these people." Morrison pointed a finger at the screen. "But she's the wild card. I don't trust her at all."

Leroux stared at the red-coated woman as she sprayed gunfire at her own people while all four of them sprinted toward the main gate. If she wasn't on their side, she was playing the part extremely well.

En route to Rendezvous Point

North Korean Waters

Chan had been given a crash course on how to pilot the boat, and had practiced for several days. He had the hang of it, but the water was a little choppy and it was now fairly dark. For the moment, he had every light off and the engine at full throttle as he pushed the small fishing craft toward the North Korean coast and the rendezvous point. He had received the signal only minutes ago, which meant the escape had begun. He had thanked every deity he could think of for getting the ball rolling sooner rather than later, but most of the options he now faced weren't good.

Kane could already be dead, or he might never make the rendezvous. Or worse, a North Korean patrol could capture him in their waters. Depending on how good his bullshitting skills were, he could find himself in a prison camp or worse. But he had his story. It was believable, but things had to go perfectly for him to make it out of here alive.

He thought of his wife and the day they had met, then pictured her as he had last seen her only days ago. Those who didn't know her would say the years hadn't been kind to her, but to those who would say such a thing, he would say that in his eyes, she was even more beautiful than that first day. He squeezed his eyes shut and fought the burn as a lump formed in his throat.

Damn you, Kane. If you get me killed and she's left alone, I'll never forgive you.

Nyongbyon Nuclear Scientific Research Center

Nyongbyon, North Korea

Kane tossed his assault rifle to the ground and grabbed another one off a dead body, resuming the sprint toward the main gate. The elderly Gorman was slowing them down, though not by much. He appeared to be in decent shape and motivated. Kane glanced over at Kwan, still uncertain as to whether he could trust her. She was firing on her own people, and he had paid close enough attention to confirm she was actually killing some of them. Yet this was North Korea. He would never kill an American soldier in a situation like this if the roles were reversed, but the North Koreans valued life differently.

Kane opened fire at a cluster of red coats nearby when he had a revelation—he had been targeting uniforms and red coats the entire time, picking them out of the crowd of white coats with ease. Just as his enemy was likely targeting their yellow coats. He stripped out of the lab coat and tossed it to the ground. "Take off the yellow lab coats!" he shouted to the others.

Gorman immediately stripped out of his, tossing it away with gusto, as if it had been an albatross around his neck for years. Jack shrugged out of his own as he continued to fire, and by the time they reached the main gates, Kwan was the only one wearing a lab coat in a color that shouldn't make her a target.

"To the trees!" he yelled, having spotted the muzzle flashes from Bravo Team. They rushed across the road and into the tree line as a massive explosion erupted behind them. A grenade or something similar had just taken out the guardhouse behind them, secondary explosions from the ordnance stored there putting on a spectacular show.

Somebody stepped from the trees and aimed a weapon at Kwan. "I'll have you put that down now, ma'am."

Kane stepped between Kwan and Dawson. "We're all friends here, aren't we?"

Dawson gave him a look. "Up until a few hours ago, I was here to kill you."

"Glad you didn't."

"Eh, I've disobeyed orders before, but I decided it was best to get your side of the story first."

Kane grinned and gave Dawson a thumping hug as others revealed their positions.

"As much as I'd like a good sport hump," said Niner. "We better get the hell out of here."

Dawson pointed toward the chaos. "Everybody throw two grenades then empty one more mag, and Atlas, if you've got any more rounds, fire 'em off, then we go to the bikes."

"Roger that!" echoed the team. Everyone broke and moments later gunfire erupted as grenades detonated, more panic sounding from the facility they had just escaped. They were rejoined by Bravo Team who then led them at a sprint through the near pitch-black of the forest.

They dodged in and out of the dense trees, Kane holding Kwan's hand protectively when Niner, leading them, came to a halt and yanked away some camouflage revealing an electric motorcycle.

Kane grinned. "Cool! Haven't been on one of these in ages."

Niner gave him a look. "Ages? Didn't they just like invent these things?"

Kane straddled the motorcycle and Kwan climbed on back with him. "We get the newest toys long before you grunts."

"Hey, that's my bike," protested Spock.

"Not anymore."

Dawson yanked away some camouflage netting and climbed on the bike it had been hiding. "Everybody double up. I want to be on that road in sixty seconds."

The only protest heard was when Niner tried to get on the back of Atlas' bike. The big man pushed him to the ground. "Do the math, little man."

Niner hopped on the back of Jimmy's bike and Kane turned on the engine, following Dawson through the trees then onto a dirt road. His old comrade in arms spoke into his comms, reporting in to Control, and Kane glanced over at Atlas.

"I need comms!"

Atlas reached into his vest and pulled out a spare set, handing it over.

"Take the wheel," said Kane over his shoulder, and Kwan reached forward, grabbing the handlebars as he fit his comms into place. He resumed control and she wrapped her arms around his waist, pressing her face against his back. "Control, this is Thunder Chicken. Do you read, over?"

Leroux responded immediately. "Thunder Chicken, Control Actual. I read you. Good to hear your voice, over."

"Good to be heard. Any chance Fang's with you?"

"Negative. She's visiting Bethesda."

Kane picked up on what his friend meant. "So, you figured it out. Good. I had a feeling you would. I'm going to stay off the airwaves now. This is Zero-One's op, but be advised I have one Korean national with me who is requesting asylum."

"Copy that, Thunder Chicken, Control, out."

Dawson's voice came in over Kane's new earpiece. "Control, Zero-One. Status on the road."

"Clear ahead, Zero-One. Your turn-off is in half a klick on your left. Triggering your decoy now."

USS Chicago, Los Angeles Class Submarine

Outside the 12-Mile Limit

Yellow Sea

Seaman Carl Rodriguez stood on the deck of the USS Chicago as every light the sub had and every light that could be held shone toward the North Korean coastline. It was the nuttiest thing he had ever seen in his two years serving. He turned to his best friend, Paul Simmons. "What the hell are we doing?"

Simmons shrugged. "You think they'd tell me? I'm just as low on the totem pole as you are."

"I really hope we're outside the twelve-mile limit. From what I've heard, the North Koreans can be unpredictable sometimes."

"Yeah. I don't think we want to be the next USS Pueblo."

"What the hell is that?"

Simmons laughed. "Dude, learn your history. You should know everything there is to know about where you're being deployed."

"Yeah, yeah, okay, Professor, what the hell's the Pueblo?"

"Let's just say they were taken prisoner for eleven months by the North Koreans, and I can guarantee you they weren't trying to piss them off like we are."

Rodriguez spun as a flare was launched from the opposite end of the sub. "My God, what the hell are they thinking? I thought we were here to extract somebody."

Simmons shrugged. "Maybe they're letting them know where we are."

"This is the twenty-first century, not World War Two. We've got modern comms, GPS, satellites, everything." The flare erupted overhead, brilliant blues, greens, and yellows spraying out in every direction as more were launched. "What the hell?"

Simmons raised a hand to shield his eyes slightly. "Fireworks?"

"Looks like it."

"What the hell are we launching fireworks for?"

"I don't know. Practicing for the Fourth of July?"

"*Is* it the Fourth of July? The day I step on board, I try to forget what the date is so I don't think about all the birthdays and anniversaries I'm missing."

"Anniversaries, plural? How many women have you got out there?"

Simmons grinned. "More than you'll ever have."

"You wish."

The lieutenant walked behind them and Rodriguez turned. "Lieutenant, what's going on? Why are we putting on a show?"

"Just drawing the attention of our North Korean friends."

"Friends? Did we sign a treaty that I missed?"

The lieutenant chuckled. "Not unless I missed it too. Just make sure that when they come, you've got a big smile on your face. Remember, we're all big, dumb, drunk Americans, just like they think we are."

"Well, Lieutenant, if you don't want to make liars out of them, you should be breaking out Jimmy's hooch."

The 1MC squawked and everyone fell silent. "Now hear this: enemy patrol boat approaching from the north port side. Everybody remain calm and we'll be okay. We're in international waters." The captain laughed. "Just pretend Clint Eastwood just flew off in the Firefox and we're waving to the Soviet helicopters."

Rodriguez turned to Simmons. "What the hell's a Firefox?"

"Haven't a clue. Who's Clint Eastwood?"

"No idea. Sounds made up." The roar of the patrol boat grew as it rapidly approached, heading directly for them on a collision course. "You don't think this joker is going to try to ram us, do you?"

Simmons shrugged. "I don't know. They're North Korean, so they're nuts. Just keep smiling."

Rodriguez forced a Sheldon Cooper-esque smile and Simmons elbowed him. "You're going to terrify them with that."

"To hell with them. I'm the one who's terrified."

The boat turned at the last second, sending its wash across the deck as it came to a halt, its own lights now shining at them, somebody on a loudspeaker shouting in broken English, but Rodriguez couldn't understand it through the pounding in his ears.

The captain responded. "This is Captain Ferris of the USS Chicago. We are in international waters and don't recognize your authority here. It is our Chief of the Boat's birthday, and we're celebrating. You are more than welcome to send a delegation to join us."

Rodriguez glanced at Simmons. "I didn't know it was the COB's birthday."

"I don't think he knew either."

"Why do I get the distinct impression that we're cannon fodder for somebody more important?"

"We're decoys, gentlemen," said the lieutenant from behind them. "Nothing to worry about."

"Yeah, well, sometimes they shoot the decoys."

"Just keep smiling. And if anybody asks, the Chief is fifty today and is thrilled about celebrating it in international waters."

Half a dozen assault rifles were suddenly raised and aimed at them. Rodriguez threw his hands up as did Simmons. "I don't think they want a party, Lieutenant."

Before the lieutenant could respond, half a dozen guys that looked like they were out of Call of Duty emerged from below decks, spreading across the length of the sub, their weapons aimed at the waterline of the North Korean vessel.

Rodriguez felt something warm on his leg. "I think I just pissed myself," he hissed.

Simmons grunted. "Better than what I think I just did."

Ministry of State Security Headquarters

Pyongyang, North Korea

Major Choe couldn't get the smile off his face. His team had arrived in Pyongyang several hours ago and had been debriefed, Command evidently quite happy with how the mission had turned out, though as per usual, reluctant to come right out and say it. But the fact their families were waiting for them after debriefing meant they had done well, and that the colonel was a man of his word.

His wife was as gorgeous as he remembered her, and his two little girls were so big now, it broke his heart at how much time he had missed. But thanks to what he and his team had accomplished, evenings spent in the dark could be a thing of the past.

"I've missed you so much," said his wife as she continued to hold his hand—the poor woman hadn't broken physical contact with him since the moment he stepped into the room. "You've been gone so long, why do you have to go again so soon?"

"It's the job, but I'll never be gone that long again. This is just a short-term assignment. I can't see it lasting more than a few days."

Someone rapped on the door before it burst open. "Sir, you're needed."

Choe could tell from the concern on the captain's face that it was serious. And that he wouldn't be coming back. He gave his wife a brief kiss then his daughters big hugs. "I have to go, but I'll see you soon, I promise." Tears rolled down his wife's cheeks as he closed the door and steeled for what was to come. "What's going on?"

"The Americans have escaped."

"What? How?"

"I don't know, but I've got a chopper waiting. They think they've trapped them. We found a US nuclear sub off the coast waiting for them. The colonel wants us in the area immediately."

Choe pushed through the doors, sprinting toward the chopper. "What are our orders?"

"Kill them all on sight."

Choe smiled slightly. "Killing that arrogant American will be a privilege."

Operations Center 2, CIA Headquarters

Langley, Virginia

Leroux stared at the displays showing the location of Bravo Team and the escapees, along with every moving man and vehicle in the area. It was getting crowded.

"Looks like they're taking the bait," said Child, and Leroux had to agree. The bright red dot indicating the USS Chicago was looking like a rallying point. Scores of North Korean assets, including air, ground, and naval, were all heading toward her location twelve miles offshore, firmly in international waters. The entire route ahead of Bravo Team remained clear all the way to the coast.

"This looks like it just might work." Tong grinned at him. "Smooth for a change?"

Leroux grunted. "Nobody's out of there yet, not even our sub. This can go south very fast."

Child pointed at the screen. "What do you think's going on there?"

Leroux squinted. "Where?"

"Just north of the diversion. It looks like a North Korean vessel is heading toward the rendezvous point."

Leroux cursed. "Could they have spotted the extraction vessel?"

Morrison pursed his lips. "It's possible. They might have picked it up on radar, or one of those choppers heading toward our diversion could have spotted it."

Leroux agreed. "Or just someone on shore. He's supposed to only be one klick away." He activated his comms. "Zero-One, Control. We have a North Korean vessel closing in on the rendezvous point, over."

"Copy that, Control. ETA?"

"Seven minutes."

"Understood. Zero-One, out."

"Now what do we do?" asked Child. "If they take out the rendezvous vessel, our guys are screwed."

"Then we figure out another way." Morrison headed for the door. "I'm going to talk to the Pentagon and see what options we have. This might turn into a Charlie-Foxtrot after all."

Rendezvous Point

Yellow Sea Coast, North Korea

The road abruptly ended, revealing the still dimly lit water ahead. Dawson guided them onto the beach and gunned it toward the water's edge as Kane searched for Chan. A flashlight flicked three times just to their left, and he guided them toward it, coming to a halt beside a rubber dinghy with an agitated Chan standing beside it, beckoning to them.

"Hurry up, hurry up! They could be on us any minute!" His eyes bulged at the ten people that dismounted. "Are you kidding me? What's this? I thought I was just retrieving you and maybe two others."

"I told you to prep for fifteen."

"I thought you were joking."

"That boat's going to be on us in six minutes," said Dawson. "Enough discussion."

Chan pointed at the boat. "Weakest swimmers inside. The rest of you swim for it. She's just over there." He pointed at a shadow offshore. "I brought her in as close as I could. Two hundred meters, or two kilometers doesn't matter. When you're inside their waters, you're inside their waters."

Dawson pointed at each person he wanted in the boat. "Kane, Jack, Dr. Gorman, and Kwan, I want you all on the boat. You were the mission. Atlas, go with them. You're like an anchor in the pool. The rest of you, strip down. Put your weapons in the boat."

Chan shook his head. "No weapons, no comms, nothing. If they search us and find anything or pick up a signal, we're dead."

Dawson eyed the man as everyone executed his orders. "Sir, if they search us, we're certainly dead if we don't have weapons."

Chan looked at Kane. "Didn't you tell them the plan?"

Kane shrugged. "Hasn't really been much time." He helped Kwan into the boat then climbed in after her. "Let's just get moving."

Dawson tossed his weapons on the pile of clothes. "Tuck your locator beacons in your shorts, just in case this goes south."

Chan cursed at Dawson then gunned the engine, directing them out toward the boat as the others plunged into the chilly water. Chan was right. He had brought it in almost to the shoreline. They reached the fishing vessel just as the North Korean patrol boat rounded the bend and came into sight. Chan tied them off and climbed up on the deck, then pointed to the water. "The gear's where you wanted it. Just stay out of sight."

Kane gave the man a thumbs-up. "Good luck!"

"To us all. Now go!"

"Everybody in the drink." Kane was met with three stunned stares. "Into the water, now!" He jumped over first and the rest reluctantly followed as the roar of the patrol boat neared. "Take a deep breath and follow me. There's oxygen below."

"What the hell are you talking about?" asked Jack.

"Trust me." Kane took a deep breath and broke the surface then kicked, guiding himself along the hull until he found what he was searching for—two dozen oxygen canisters strapped to the hull. He yanked one free and handed it to Dr. Gorman, fitting it into the man's mouth. Gorman's eyes widened as he took his first tentative breath, then gave a thumbs-up as the others yanked their own canisters from the bottom of the boat. Kane pointed at the straps that had held the canisters in place then grabbed one, yanking it, indicating they should hold on to them should the boat move. Everyone acknowledged the instructions then he pointed at his chest then the surface.

He grabbed five canisters, tucking them into his shirt, then kicked off the hull, heading toward where Bravo Team should be. They didn't have far to swim and should be close, but the North Korean patrol was almost on top of them, and he had to get them off the surface. If he knew Dawson, he would have them stop and tread water, out of sight of the spotlights that would now be on the boat.

He kept below the surface, swimming back toward the shore, when he spotted his first set of feet. He fished a canister out from his shirt then, rather than startle whoever it was by touching them, he instead pushed the canister up in front of their face. They grabbed it, fit it in place, and dropped below the surface. It was Niner. Kane handed him two of the canisters and they soon had all five Bravo Team members underwater, breathing easy.

Using hand signals, Kane guided them back to the boat, and within minutes everyone was hanging on to the bottom of the fishing vessel as shouts erupted from above, their lives now all dependent on whatever performance Chan could muster.

If Chan hadn't already taken a piss off the deck fifteen minutes ago, he'd be soiling himself right now. His hands were poker straight in the air as at least half a dozen weapons, including a .50 cal, were aimed directly at him. This was it. This could be the end of his life or the most exciting story he would ever tell. This was never supposed to be his job. He was supposed to be a courier. Documents would be delivered to him, and he'd pass them on. He'd provide equipment to operatives, provide them a safe haven.

But over the years, he had slowly got drawn in, and now here he was, not only putting his own life on the line, but the next few moments could determine the fate of the ten people he hoped were now hiding underneath his vessel. The patrol craft bumped up against his and half a dozen men rushed on board, followed by a lieutenant.

"Why are you in our waters?"

Chan pointed toward the motor. "My fuel line broke, so I drifted in. I'm really sorry."

"Your fuel line broke? You don't have a spare?"

"Spares cost money, and fishing doesn't pay like it used to."

The lieutenant snapped something, and judging by what happened next, it was orders to search the boat. Chan shook, putting on the show without needing to act. This was the most terrified he'd been in his entire life.

"Papers!"

Chan handed over his identification and fishing license, and the lieutenant passed them to someone on the boat who disappeared inside. The search took less than ten minutes and was no doubt thorough based on the amount of banging and smashing. Negative reports were acknowledged by the lieutenant. The lieutenant stepped back onto the patrol boat and disappeared inside the cabin for several minutes as Chan's knees knocked uncontrollably. He reappeared and stepped back on board, handing over the papers.

"It appears you are who you say you are."

"Of course, sir. I would never lie to you."

Another man stepped on board with a toolkit. "Our mechanic is going to fix your fuel line."

Chan forced a beaming smile, praising himself for not simply cutting the line with a knife. "That would be wonderful, sir. You are too kind. I wish there was some way this old fisherman could repay you."

"Just carry spare parts next time."

The mechanic disappeared below and he prayed that those hiding underneath remained silent. Just a single boot colliding with the hull would be instantly noticed by the mechanic as something that shouldn't be. The engine roared to life and the mechanic reemerged with a smile.

He handed Chan the broken fuel line, the fuel line he had carefully sabotaged just before coming to shore. He said something in Korean.

Chan shrugged. "Sorry?"

"Rats," translated the lieutenant.

"What?"

"He said he thinks rats chewed your line."

Chan spat on the deck. "Vile creatures. I'll kill every one of them."

"See that you do." The lieutenant stepped back on his boat, snapping an order that had him soon followed by the rest of his crew. The North Koreans pulled away and Chan smiled and waved at them before returning to the pilothouse and gently applying the throttle as he banked to starboard, guiding them toward international waters. The patrol boat was soon out of sight and Chan cranked it. It would be rough for those below, but he had to put as much distance as he could between the shoreline and himself. Twelve miles or twenty kilometers would take time in an old wreck like this with ten people not only weighing it down, but dragging it down.

He rushed back to the railing and hurled one more time.

Yellow Sea, International Waters

Choe stared out from the chopper at the scene below. A US sub was sitting in what he was told were international waters, and three patrol boats now surrounded her. No shots had been fired yet, but the briefing he had received in the air told him something was wrong. Kane had played them from the beginning. He still wasn't sure what was happening, but Major Pak indicated he had been taken down expertly by Burkett, which suggested Burkett wasn't a scientist at all, but another CIA operative.

The most disturbing part was that Kwan appeared to be working with them. How that was even possible, he had no idea. His briefing told him she was an intelligence asset trained for companionship who had never been out of the country. How Kane could have recruited her and then how Command could have selected her simply made no sense. This suggested to him the possibility she was pretending to go along, or she was exploiting the opportunity to defect herself.

The chaos at the nuclear plant had been caused by outside forces, which meant a special forces team had been sent in to rescue Kane rather than kill him. It indicated a well-coordinated op, and there was no way an operation planned so perfectly would have an exfil done by a submarine lit up with fireworks like it was a party.

"This is a decoy," he said, turning to the captain. "There's no way this is the rendezvous point." He leaned forward and pointed ahead. "Head north along the coastline."

"Yes, major." The chopper dipped forward and they left the distraction behind. Every asset in the area was converging on that sub. Unfortunately, the diversion had likely worked. By his calculations, the Americans would have already reached the shore and met whatever vessel they were to rendezvous with in secrecy. The pilot banked slightly to the right as he followed the coastline, and a patrol vessel came into sight.

"See if you can raise them on the radio."

"Yes, sir." The pilot put out the call and it was immediately responded to.

"Ask him if he's spotted anything unusual in the past fifteen minutes." The question was relayed and the pilot shook his head at the response.

"Nothing, sir, just a Chinese fishing trawler with a broken fuel line that they helped get underway."

Choe cursed. "That's it! Find out where they headed and tell them to intercept."

"Yes, sir."

Choe turned to the captain. "I bet a month's rations that they're on that trawler. We might just get them yet."

Operations Center 2, CIA Headquarters

Langley, Virginia

High fives and hugs were exchanged around the room as the satellite image showed the patrol boat leaving Chan's vessel, then Chan heading for international waters. There was still no sign of Delta or Kane's foursome since they had disappeared under the water, but they had pinged the locator beacons for Bravo Team, and they showed they were clustered on the boat somehow. Where they were hidden or how they had gotten aboard, he had no clue, because the North Koreans appeared to have performed a thorough search.

"Could they still be underwater?" asked Child. "I mean, there's no way you hide ten people on a boat that size. It's not like he can put them in a hidden closet. You'd have to put them in a hidden ballroom."

"Chan wouldn't say what the plan was when Fang spoke to him. I don't think he entirely trusted her or that their communications weren't being monitored. How long before they're in international waters?"

Tong brought the estimate up on the main display. "At least forty minutes. That thing's not exactly a race boat. The North Koreans have to figure out that it's just a diversion soon. I don't think we have forty minutes."

Child cursed. "Neither do I." He pointed at the displays. "Is it my imagination or did that patrol boat just turn around after that helicopter flew over?"

Everyone stared and Leroux cursed. He reached for his comms before remembering that everything had been abandoned on shore. "ETA?"

Tong sighed. "Less than fifteen minutes for the boat, five for the chopper. There's no way they're going to make it."

Yellow Sea, North Korean Territorial Waters

Kane clung to the bottom of the boat along with the others. So far, thankfully, none of the handholds had failed, but if this kept on much longer, one of them might be forced to let go out of fatigue, and his money was on Dr. Gorman, who appeared to be struggling. Kane signaled to Atlas, closest to the elderly man, and Atlas reached out with his free hand and grabbed the man by the belt, providing him with some support and some much-needed relief.

Kane took the opportunity to switch hands, which had him rolling back toward Kwan. He couldn't figure her out. She had had multiple opportunities to sabotage their escape, yet she hadn't. But she knew the truth, that it had all been an act, that there was no real bond beyond what two people sharing what they had would naturally create.

Yet she had helped them anyway. It had to be that she had recognized an opportunity for a better life and was taking it, and if that were the case, he couldn't fault her. What ended up happening to her was above his pay grade. Washington and Langley would decide what would become of her. She could be granted asylum and live out her life in exile like Fang, or she could be a double agent, taking the opportunity to insert herself as instructed by Pyongyang.

Definitely above his pay grade.

Her eyes smiled at him and she reached out with her free hand, taking his and squeezing it. Then her eyes widened with fear as she let go. He gave her a questioning look and she pointed at her ear. He listened and his heart sank at the sound of a larger boat approaching, and any doubt as to its intention was eliminated the moment Chan cut his engine, revealing another more ominous sound.

Helicopter rotors.

I guess we're not getting away with it after all.

This time, Chan did piss his pants as the patrol boat once again pulled up beside him, this time accompanied by a chopper, its rotors pounding overhead. "Sir, is there a problem?" he asked the lieutenant, whose demeanor was far gruffer this time.

"Where are they?"

"Where are who?"

"The Americans!"

Chan stared at him, puzzled. "What Americans? I'm a fisherman. You searched the boat already. You know I'm alone."

The search team disappeared below decks, once again tearing the place apart.

"I know you're lying to me. Where have you hidden them?"

Chan shrugged, his hands still raised high. "I don't know what I can tell you. There are no Americans here. There's nobody here. There's just me."

"Then why were you going so fast?"

Chan's eyes bulged. "If you were a lowly fisherman and found yourself in foreign waters, wouldn't you go as fast as you could to get back home?"

The lieutenant regarded him for a moment, saying nothing, when the search team emerged from below, again empty-handed. The lieutenant stared up at the chopper above and shook his head. Chan was still within North Korean waters. Nobody could help them unless they were willing to break international law, and if they stayed here much longer, those hitching a ride below would run out of oxygen.

An idea occurred to him. The Delta team had kept their locator beacons, against his wishes, but it presented an opportunity.

"Sir, I realize something must be going on if you're looking for Americans. Trust me, I hate them as much as you do. If you need to satisfy your superiors, take me into custody. Take my boat if you need to and tear it apart on shore so your superiors know you and your men missed nothing."

The lieutenant regarded him for a moment as he no doubt mulled the offer, yet even he had to know there was no way they missed ten people, which is when he realized there was no way the man could know how many were hiding. The most he would know about is four, and then perhaps surmise that others had helped. And with the way the

North Koreans worked, they might not have revealed to the lower echelon how many were involved at all.

The chopper overhead abruptly banked away, the lights that had been shining down on them dimming the area slightly. But more importantly, the absence of the thundering rotors allowed them to hear another sound, causing everyone to turn.

Chan gulped, and if he had anything left in his bladder, it would have released. The lieutenant cursed and hopped back on his boat as his men followed in a panic, its engine gunning as it beat a hasty retreat from the massive American destroyer now approaching, fully lit, with all of its weapons aimed at the patrol boat. Chan waved at them as the ship's engines kicked into reverse, rapidly killing its speed.

I really wish I hadn't pissed myself.

USS Higgins

Yellow Sea

Kane stepped into the rec room of the USS Higgins, an Arleigh Burke-class destroyer, freshly showered and shaved, wearing a set of clothes provided by the US Navy. He'd already had a tearful video conference reunion with Fang that had gone far better than he expected, though she might kill him in his sleep tomorrow night when they reunited in person. Kwan was already under guard in secure quarters, and would be transferred to Busan as soon as they put into port, where she promised to reveal the location of Gorman's family once her freedom was assured. He would likely never see her again. He had paid her a visit, apologizing, and she seemed to have accepted it.

"Why did you help us?"

"Because I wanted to see America. I wanted to see freedom."

It was as reasonable an explanation as any. She would have been trained to make people like him comfortable. It meant exposure to his culture and his beliefs, and perhaps that was enough for one to question one's loyalties. He prayed that she was being honest with him, and that if she were, the powers that be would recognize it and give her the life everyone deserved, no matter what flag they were born under.

He dropped onto a couch, one end occupied by Jack. A good chunk of Bravo Team was scattered about the room reserved for the ship's guests. "So, I assume Jack here has brought you up to speed?"

Dawson nodded. "Yeah. You guys are nuts."

"Pretty ballsy," said Niner. "You realize I had the shot?"

Kane regarded him. "But you didn't take it."

"Only because Atlas didn't have his, then when he did, he recognized Jack."

"Well, thank God for that."

Jack grinned. "I am good to have around sometimes. And this pretty face is hard to forget."

Atlas groaned. "Oh, God, all you CIA types are the same. You're in love with yourselves."

Jack gave him a look. "Buddy, if you were as good-looking as us, you'd be in love with yourself too."

Kane fist-bumped him.

Atlas flexed a massive bicep. "Call me when you're as jacked as this."

Jack's head bobbed. "Respect."

Kane sighed and closed his eyes as he stretched his arms out on the back of the couch. "I feel like we've forgotten something."

Spock cocked an eyebrow. "Did we lose count?"

Niner made a show of a head count they all were making.

Kane shook his head. "No, it's something else."

"Person, place, or thing?" asked Niner.

"Thing. Some *thing* we've forgotten."

Niner leaped to his feet, excitement on his face. "Ooh, I forgot the hole check."

Everybody groaned and Kane eyed him. "I don't think I want to know what the hell you're talking about."

Dawson shook his head. "Trust me, you don't."

Jimmy batted a hand. "Just stop thinking about it and you'll remember." He pointed at the television screen playing on mute. "That can't be a good combination."

"What's that?" asked Kane.

"A British sports car known for its bad electrical systems becoming an electric vehicle."

Kane chuckled.

I guess we didn't forget anything after all.

THE END

ACKNOWLEDGMENTS

Who is #10?

If you are a hockey fan, then you probably know who Guy Lafleur was. He was one of the greatest hockey players of all time, and from all accounts, an even greater guy off the ice. He played most of his career with the Montreal Canadiens. When I was a kid, they were my team, since the only choices were them or Toronto, and my dad was a Habs (Les Habitants) fan.

Yes, all these names are for the same team. You figure it out, I can't.

I remember watching him fly down the ice, his long hair flowing, because back then most of them didn't wear helmets. And surprise, surprise, they kept their sticks down a lot more than today. I never did get to see him play in person, which is too bad, but I'll never forget watching him.

Unfortunately, he passed while I was writing this book, and it affected me more than I would have expected. You know you're getting old when your heroes start to die.

The musicians, actors, writers, and sports heroes I grew up with have either already passed, or are getting to that age when many of them could be tomorrow's headline. Every single author I read as a child is dead, though I read a lot of classic sci-fi, so most of them were gone already. Many of the musicians have either passed, given up touring (or should), or are on their final tours.

I've been a KISS fan since I was seven years old. They're on their final tour. I only saw them once when they reunited and put the makeup back on, and it was one of the greatest concerts of my life. I would love to see them one more time, but my health won't allow it—the pain would ruin the experience, and I'd rather have that treasured memory from years ago to remember them by.

When your heroes die, you can sometimes question your own mortality. Clint Eastwood, Harrison Ford, Paul Stanley, Gene Simmons, Wayne Gretzky. The list goes on, and they're all much older than me.

I'm not looking forward to the day I wake up to hear the next hero has died.

On another note, where I live was hit by a derecho. Never heard of it? Neither had I. If you have, apply to get on Jeopardy. Do it now. You'll win. For the rest of us, a derecho is essentially a sustained, widespread windstorm. People are dead, power is out for over 100,000 people, traffic lights are out, trees are down, and much more. I've been hit hard the last two storms we had in this area. The last microburst took my roof, and the last tornado took my fence. I'm happy to be safe with no damage and power that's still on, though I was disappointed it didn't take my deck—it's due to be replaced.

It did mean the birthday plans I made with my daughter had to be canceled. Have you ever eaten an entire cake by yourself? I recommend not doing it in one sitting!

As usual, there are people to thank. My dad for all the research, Dave Brooklyn for some motorcycle info (ape hangers!), Brent Richards for some weapons info, Greg "Chief" Michael for some submarine info, and, as always, my wife, daughter, my late mother who will always be an angel on my shoulder as I write, as well as my friends for their continued support, and my fantastic proofreading team!

To those who have not already done so, please visit my website at www.jrobertkennedy.com, then sign up for the Insider's Club to be notified of new book releases. Your email address will never be shared or sold.

Thank you once again for reading.

Made in the USA
Monee, IL
29 December 2022

23927371R10187